UNTO THIS MOUNTAIN

The ArchAngel Missions
BOOK V

JOSHUA LOYD FOX

Published by Watertower Hill Publishing, LLC

Cover and internal artwork by Susan Roddey at The Snark Shop by Pheonix and Fae Creations.

Author's Note
All character and names in this book are fictional and are not designed, patterned after, nor descriptive of any person, living or deceased.
Any similarities to people, living or deceased is purely by coincidence. Author and Publisher are not liable for any likeness described herein.

Library of Congress Control Number: 2023112233

ISBN: 979-8-9893011-7-1

This book is dedicated to:
The men and women of Cal Farley's Boys Ranch, and my
fellow brothers and sisters from there.
Everything I know about being good and decent in this
world, I learned from my years at the Ranch.
Thank you all for the lessons, and the memories.

Joshua Loyd Daughrity (Fox)
MF-108
MF Home, 1992-1997

*"Have faith………For verily I say unto you, that whosoever
shall say unto this mountain, Be thou removed, and be thou
cast into the sea………he shall have whatsoever he saith."*

Mark 11:22-23 (abridged) KJV

And in the Days of End,

where Veil was torn,

and ungodly swarm

tore at Creator's Horde,

Book of the Tower and the Traitor—Strophe Five

Prologue

The ArchAngel Raguel was simply at a loss for words. *Severely unlike him*, Gabriel thought to himself.

Gabriel kept his thoughts locked within his own Aura, not allowing his fellow Brother in the Elder Ilk to know what he was thinking, or how comical he thought the entire ordeal was.

Raguel looked down on the world below and sighed deep within his dark pale blue Aura. His light dimmed momentarily, and he sighed again. He did not want this Mission.

Gabriel slapped him on the back harder than he meant to. He knew exactly how Raguel felt. But this Mission was directly tied to Raguel's Aspect, and therefore, the Mission fell to him.

Raguel sighed deeply again, using air that did not exist within the Spiritual Plane, and corporeal lungs that didn't need to breathe.

Old habits die hard.

"Redemption rather than Justice on this one, eh, Brother?" Raguel looked up into the deep golden countenance of the oldest of the ArchAngels.

Gabriel simply nodded.

"So be it." Raguel sighed again. He simply nodded and prepared the way.

The ArchAngel Raguel wasn't looking forward to this Mission, after so much fighting and confusion with the encroachment of the *Antithesis*.

The entire Host was outraged, always looking over their angelic shoulders for another attack.

Every time they settled into a different world for a Mission, they were attacked, and it was becoming increasingly difficult to enact the Father's Will. But it had to be done.

The entire Celestial Creation was at stake. Every single Plane. Every single creature. Even the Host itself.

"So be it, indeed," Gabriel muttered under his breath as Raguel winked out of the Spiritual and appeared in the Material.

The ArchAngel Gabriel watched as his Brother, in his human guise, winked into existence in the bedroom of a lovely, red-haired young woman, and smiled slightly as Raguel bent over the sleeping form and whispered something in her ear.

And where the Creator would have historically been watching over his Children enacting the Mission He had set before them, there was only silence and solitude.

The Creator was nowhere to be found, in all of the Heavens, and all of the Earths, and the Host was left wondering what would become of them all.

On the eve of the greatest battle the Host had yet seen with the Anthesis, the Creator was nowhere to be found. *And without Him*, Gabriel thought, worry marring his Golden Aura, *they were all doomed.*

Part 1

The Past Always Comes 'Round Knocking

Chapter 1

Gavin Malloy sat horseback, looking down at the sprawling ranch spread out below the plateau under his painted mare's hooves, and likened his acreage to a checkerboard of greens and tans.

He sighed deeply, feeling in his soul contentment and ease. The first such feeling he'd had in more years than he cared to admit. But it didn't last long.

It never did.

Sudden, harsh flashes of memory, colorful in their intensity, seared into his consciousness, but he tamped them down like putting out a smoldering fire with his cow-leather boots on.

He quieted the sounds of gunshots, the splatter of blood and viscera, and the sights in his mind's eye of bodies strown about on dirty streets and amidst scrub brush and trail dust.

It was hard to do, as years of death and destruction at his own hands tried to burrow their way into his consciousness, but he damped them down with a fierce determination.

He learned a long time ago to not let those specific memories take over his mind.

His American Paint mare, brown-and-white-colored coat like a pool of spilled paint, shook her head impatiently beneath him, causing him to smile and pat her multi-colored mane with his gloved hand.

He got the point and pulled her reins to the right, moving her back down the trail they had climbed together a few moments before.

She obeyed the reins like she always did, with her normal air of exasperation and a simple 'putting up with' for the man atop her.

"Shhh, Mabel, I know it's hot," he told the mare on the way down the narrow, rocky path.

Mabel simply shook her mane again, jostling him in the saddle. The familiar movement made him smile, but the smile never reached his eyes.

He enjoyed coming up to the top of this rocky ridge with the mare, being able to look down into the valley his ranch lay within and get a birds-eye view of what the good lord had given him when he knew he deserved next to nothing.

And that thought, heavy in his mind once again, stayed with him all the way back down to the hot, sun-soaked valley floor, and back to a world of hard labor and small profits.

Soon after his morning ride up to the top of the ridge, Gavin stood in the large pole barn at the south end of his homestead, throwing bales of hay down from the holding loft, to be used in the cow pastures to the west, when his brother Colt limped in, hell bent on getting Gavin's attention.

But first, they both had to admire the perfect rectangles of hay, held tightly with twine, that the modern technology Gavin had purchased earlier in the spring made.

The bales sure as hell beat having loose hay and straw lying in piles all over the pole barn.

"You know, we can store twice as much hay in the loft with these bales than we could with the loose," Gavin told his older brother.

Colt, not long on words, simply nodded.

He was pleased with the bale presser as well. But it had taken more than a month to get the jumpy horses to walk on the wood and leather 'treadmill' that powered the damn thing.

Gavin smiled at the large pile of bales in the upper reaches of the barn, thinking the same thing.

It was hot as a gunny sack in the barn, but both men were excited about the innovative technology. The power of the future had them both thinking of things other than what had brought Colt to the barn to bend his brother's ear.

"Got the post in a few minutes ago." Colt's long, drawling voice sounded more gravelly than it did most days. *Must have gotten into the whiskey the night before*, Gavin thought to himself.

But that thought was unfair, and he let it go.

"What'd we get?" Gavin asked, brushing straw dust off his hands and walking to the canteen lying against the wall near the big double doors of the large, wooden barn.

Taking a slow, deep swallow of the cool well water made Gavin's parched throat feel instantly better. He handed the canteen to Colt and watched as his brother took a similarly satisfying drink of the cool water as well.

Sweat lined the straw hats they both wore, and Gavin took an old rag out of the back pocket of his canvas pants to wipe his brow.

"Well, Gavin, that there's the thing," Colt was saying as he placed the canteen stopper back into the hole it went to.

"We got all the normal things, but we also got a white envelope with yer name on it. I didn't open it. Seemed important though, heavy," he said.

That was different, Gavin thought again. Colt wouldn't normally have walked all the way from the main house to tell him about an errant piece of mail.

He'd have waited until supper to give the envelope to him.

"You think it's from the Army, don't you?" Gavin asked.

Darkness seemed to settle in the barn. Both brothers knew what a letter from the Army would mean.

"Hell, I reckon, Gavin," Colt said.

The older Malloy brother looked down at his boots, and anywhere else other than his little brother's eyes.

They both breathed a deep sigh. Memories tried to push into both men's minds, but the barn, the hay, and the heat all helped them keep the worst at bay.

"Well," Gavin said, "better go see what it is, then."

Later on, looking back down the long road of memories at the scene of him and Colt in the barn that late morning, he would wish like hell he had just kept on working.

Chapter 2

Gavin could almost feel his brother's breath against the back of his neck as they walked into the dark, stuffy interior of the large, whitewashed home they had built a year earlier. He turned and gave Colt a dirty look that the older man didn't see. Or at least, if he did see it, he ignored it.

The unassuming envelope was sitting flat on the long wooden table that the boys had inherited from their mother.

Gavin approached it like it was a viper barely seen in tall grass. He figured it would bite him, in one way or another.

He took a deep breath, squared his shoulders, and picked it up. He looked back once at Colt, who took a seat on the arm of their father's old, battered lounge chair.

Colt simply nodded toward his younger brother and waited patiently for the news the envelope held.

As Gavin tore open the heavy paper of the white envelope with one finger, he felt the air in the gloomy room settle in, hot as it always was in the depths of the summer. He could hardly wait to get back out in the sun, where at least there was fresh air and a slight breeze.

He pulled the single sheet of white parchment from the envelope and saw only two lines of handwriting, scrawled deeply into the paper, like the author was trying to express his anger and fear with simple lines.

Gavin Malloy: General Ulysses Harrison requests a meeting with you the afternoon of July the 18th, 1870, at the Dorsey train station, in Dorsey, Montana. Your attention to a grave situation would be much appreciated.

It was signed by Lt. General Walter Mondaulk, who had been the aide-de-camp to General Harrison for as long as the brothers had known their former commanding officer in the Union Army.

Having been from the old Dakota Territory, the former area of land the brothers had been raised upon, did not make them favorites of the general.

That, and never being really good at following orders from the old man.

More confusion came from the letter than answers, but that was the way of the Army, both Gavin and Colt knew.

But another thing they both knew, as Gavin finished reading the short letter out loud to his brother, was that it would take nothing short of the end of the world for General Ulysses Harrison to reach out to either of the Malloy brothers.

Gavin looked over at Colt and did some quick calculations in his head. If they left the next day, they could get to Dorsey the day before the general's train was set to arrive.

They knew that the general was coming in on the train the very day of the scheduled meeting, arriving from the west, and he would probably be leaving on the same train the next day, when it made its turnabout deeper in the Montana Territory, and headed back west.

That gave the general about a day to meet with the Brothers Malloy. A proposition that neither man relished.

Gavin walked over to the sink in the kitchen of the home and pumped the tap. The warm gush soon turned cooler as the pump pulled water from the ranch's deep wells.

The winter runoff from the Long Mountain steams still ran cold. He took down a cup, blew out some dust, and filled it up with the cool water.

As he took a deep swallow of the water, Gavin's mind started figuring out the logistics of the eighty-odd mile trek they would have to take to get to Dorsey on time.

The meeting was set for the following Monday, and it being Friday this day, they would have to load up, saddle the horses, get their gear together, and ride out by Saturday morning latest.

They could get into the small town on Sunday, get a room at the single hotel/saloon there, and be freshest for their meeting.

Being well rested and bathed before meeting the general made more sense to Gavin than did the cryptic letter. *What urgent matter?* he wondered.

Colt wondered the same thing as he pondered seeing the old man again after their legendary, and explosive, parting at the slow, winding-down conclusion of the War.

He also wondered if he was still on the hook for a court martial after socking the general straight in the nose and hightailing it out of Washington with his brother, the military police hot on their trail.

Gavin looked over at his older brother, sighed mightily, and said what they were both thinking.

"Well, we better get moving, and face it like men."

Colt simply nodded.

Later that night, as the ranch house sat quietly in the stillness, as the dark, cool temperatures of the Montana summer night settled the timber wood of the frame house in small, slight popping noises, the inhabitants rested in their deepening slumber, and Gavin Malloy had a dream.

Gavin rode atop a charging, pale white mare galloping at full speed. In one hand in held the reins of the runaway horse, in the other, one of his oft-used and always reliable Remington Model 1858 revolvers. He always carried four pistols on his person, allowing others to use rifles and sniper long guns around him.

He charged full speed at a running man, closing in on him, less than thirty yards away and to his right. The man looked back while he was running, and Gavin could see the terror and pain on the man's sweaty face.

That didn't stop Gavin from doing what he did next.

The horse's hoofbeats pounded loudly in both men's ears, and as the screams of the running man died to the wind,

Gavin rode his white mare so close that he could swear afterward he smelled the terrified man's sweat.

As Gavin's horse caught up to the man in a matter of seconds, Gavin fired, practically point blank, a .44 caliber slug burying itself in the very center of the back of the man's head.

And as the man fell under the hooves of Gavin's charging horse, blood and brain matter spraying across his horse's front flanks, Gavin could feel the smile creep onto his face.

For he knew another assignment, another mission, had been accomplished by the most successful bounty-hunter in Union Army history.

Gavin awoke in his own dank sweat, the darkness of the still house pressing in, almost strangling him. He could swear the sound of his revolver's shot echoed in his ears, and in his memory.

They were a nightly occurrence, these dreams of the past, which made Gavin wish for the sweet oblivion and sweeter quiet of a peaceful death, the kind of death that he had not given to so many assignments during the terrible four years he had volunteered for the Union Army.

And the thoughts of the terribly sweet quiet of the fateful day Gavin himself would meet his end lulled him back to a fitful, restless sleep.

Chapter 3

The next morning was a misery of rain, unseasonal chill, and fog rolling in off of the mountains to the north of the Malloy Ranch. Gavin's mood matched the weather.

He swung a thick-booted foot up into the stirrups and pulled himself into the saddle atop Mable. He would trust no other horse than the old mare. She had been through most of the Civil War with the decorated soldier, and he didn't see any reason that should change now.

Colt was mounting his roan stallion in the front yard of the ranch's main house, right next to his little brother, and as Gavin got his bearings sitting his saddle, his bedroll and leather saddle bags full of supplies under him, he saw the bloodshot eyes and general lethargy of his big brother and knew that there would be few words on the trail south to their rendezvous with their court martial.

He pulled the reins over top of the saddle horn under him, and looked down on Porter, a young man that had somehow become family to the two Brothers Malloy.

The dark-skinned youth had tagged along with the brothers on a single excursion of only a few miles around the middle of the war, and they had not been able to lose the boy since.

Porter was a great hand on the ranch, however, and had proven himself worthy of inclusion into the family. Even if he had to put up with bullying from both Colt and Gavin. It was all out of fun and fondness for the boy, but they would never come right out and say it.

"Make sure to feed the steers in the back forty half rations through this month. They need to be lean before we drive them to market in the fall," he told the young man.

Porter simply nodded. He knew the workings of the cattle ranch better than Gavin himself.

"And keep your pistols strapped, Porter," he warned the boy.

"Those Blackfeet youngins' have been harassing the milk cows again," he continued.

"A black scalp is as good as a white 'un." Colt said his first words of the morning, a general ribbing of the young boy.

"Keep practicing your ropin' too, young man," Gavin admonished the youth. "I don't want to see you pulled from the saddle again after necking another steer."

Porter simply smiled and nodded, pulling his straw hat down closer on his head.

"We'll be back in a week, or we won't," Gavin told the boy. "If we are gone longer than a month, go to the camps and get Heath Kirkeby, and then the papers are in the kitchen cupboard that'll transfer deed over to you and him," Gavin said.

The brothers had no idea what awaited them in Dorsey, but they had to make sure the ranch stayed in friendly hands. *Used to be*, Gavin thought as he trotted out of the yard, *the world was too big to worry about folks bothering a ranch in the middle of nowhere, Montana Territory.*

But the world was getting a lot smaller lately, he told himself as he and Colt rode through the pass to the south of their valley and didn't look back once.

It was not the Malloy way to look back or to miss the home they had built over the last five years with the blood of their hands and the sweat of their brow.

Midday, and miles south of their ranch, the brothers stopped to eat some jerked beef, and refilled their canteens in a bubbling brook that meandered east to west.

The weather had broken as they climbed out of the foothills in the middle south of Montana, and it was starting to get hotter than a witch's tit. Gavin was glad for the cool water, though Colt seemed just as miserable as he always did after blacking out the night before.

Gavin knew the whiskey drowned out the memories, and hell, he had fallen asleep the same way a time or two, but he was worried about his big brother. It was becoming a nightly thing, Colt blacking out with the whiskey bottle still in his hand, with the fire dying low before him.

The sun beat down on the two brothers, and they took a rest under a shade tree as they let the horses graze. The mare and roan happily drank from the clean brook as well, and Gavin, despite the heat and the general discontent of his brother, was secretly glad to be back on the trail again. Even if, this time, he had only a meeting to hunt.

He looked over at his brother, who was laying back, his shoulders and head resting against the tall cottonwood tree, with his straw hat pulled down over his eyes, and sighed deeply. This wasn't going to be pretty.

"Colt, reckon we should be doing this?" he asked his older brother.

Colt simply pushed his hat up off his eyes and looked over at Gavin. He gave him the same look that he had been giving the younger Malloy for all his life. It was a look that brooked no nonsense and told Gavin to straighten himself up.

Colt simply looked at his brother, sighed, and pulled the hat back down over his eyes. After a time, he muttered the only words Gavin would hear from the older Malloy for the rest of the day.

"Tired of looking over my shoulder, little brother," he told Gavin.

The rough and windburned face of the younger Malloy took on a gentler look, and he simply took the words for what they were.

Exactly what he himself had been thinking all along.

That evening, as the air turned chilly and the moon rose in the east, both brothers bunked down in a dense field of tall limestone boulders. The large rocks cut any wind that would chill the cowboys through the night, and any dancing shadows from the small fire they built in the lee side of an extremely large bolder would stay with them and not be seen by any enemies that might be out on the open plains to the south.

Enemies like the Blackfeet warriors, scourges of the Montana Territory, that still felt it a rite of passage to bring back white men's scalps to their tribal camps, usually without the heads attached.

And the Brothers Malloy liked their scalps right where they were, thank you very much.

Gavin settled down, trying to find a comfortable spot for his sore rump after a full day in the saddle. It had been years since he had been on the trail. The rolled bedroll under him didn't keep the rocks and hard ground from grinding into his tired bones.

They would get into town the next day and have a chance to sleep in a comfortable bed and clean up. Gavin looked forward to that time, and it made sleeping on the ground in the chilly night easier.

But he had a strong feeling, that he couldn't quite put a finger on, that sleeping in a comfortable bed the next night, and after a hot bath… he had better enjoy it.

Because he was feeling with all his soul that it would be the last time he would be comfortable for a long, long while.

On the other side of the fire, his back to the world and his brother, Colt's mind was on whiskey, old memories, and the knowledge that his life, and what he had learned to lean on, rely on, and trust, was soon going to end in a blaze of glory.

Because he knew something the rest of the world didn't know.

Colt Malloy was not going to go down without a fight.

Both brothers' eyes soon shut on the world, and rest entered their tired, sore bodies.

As the fire died down between them, allowing the chill of the northern summer night to seep in, a large, robed ArchAngel looked down on the scene from atop the giant limestone boulder.

Raguel looked down on the men whose very lives were on the verge of changing, and while both men deserved death and punishment for their lives spent in dealing out the same to others, the command had come down from up high to allow these men redemption.

So be it, the ArchAngel thought to himself as he winked out of the Physical Plane and appeared in the In-Between place to continue the fight against the darkness encroaching on the two brothers from the now ever-present darkness trying to stop the Missions, and therefore, the lives of the Brothers Malloy.

With twin Diamond-Steel maces twirling like tornados, Raguel joined the battle ringing loudly through all of creation, knowing the brothers could not hear, nor perceive, the very battle for their lives, happening around the serene scene in the southern Montana Territory. Raguel fought to assure that the brothers continued moving toward their purposes, and their own redemptive story.

Chapter 4

The town of Dorsey, Montana was a new settlement that had magically appeared as the long, winding railroad was built by Irish slave labor through the wilds of virgin Dakota Territory.

When the brothers had left together to join many of their inspired neighbors and the Union Army, there had been nothing but untouched grasslands in rural southern Montana as far as the eye could see.

Major advancements after the war saw the brothers returning to their childhood home with eyes wide, hearts broken, and civilization encroaching on what had once been unmarked, and empty, open-sky territory.

Neither had been happy about it. Especially as the loud, blowing sound of the train whistle had spooked both their horses on their return home five years prior.

And here they were again, handkerchiefs pulled up over their noses and mouths to keep the dust of the rolling grasslands out of their lungs.

Both men shielded their eyes, sitting horseback in the hot sun, atop a gentle rise, looking down at the tranquil valley and sparsely dotted tree stands below.

The dark scar of the train tracks ran left to right in the very middle of the pristine, grassy valley, and Colt spit out his disgust to the side of his dark-coated stallion.

Gavin just looked down at the small town, seeing bustling crowds that had not been apparent the last time they had come through this part of the world, and looking forward to a hot bath and a soft bed.

He and Colt would find both at the only inn in all of the Southern Territory, and could put up with the crowds of cattlemen, women dressed in bright sun dresses, holding shady umbrellas, and the occasional lawman hell-bent on keeping peace in the small town built around the train station.

Hell, for a warm bath and a soft bed, some whiskey in their bellies, and maybe the favor of a lovely working girl, the boys could put up with almost anything.

This time, Gavin thought quietly to himself, *the train wasn't due until the next day, and wouldn't spook their horses as they rode down toward the dusty town.*

"Must all be here for the gold," Colt said out loud as they rode closer to the bustling town.

"Must be," Gavin agreed.

Those were the only words spoken between the brothers as they meandered into town, many townsfolk looking them up and down, giving dirty looks to the unfamiliar duo.

Gavin tipped his hat to several elegantly dressed women, and the gayly dressed men chaperoning them. But he received neither a smile nor a nod in return.

The brothers brought their horses to a halt in front of the two-story inn that sat like a blight on the earth, halfway down the main road through town and right across from the large train station. Gavin looked over at the station as he dismounted, seeing the platform empty, but grown since the years they had passed this way last.

They tied off the reins of the horses to the hitching post, grabbed their saddle bags, slung them over their shoulders, and walked with purpose into the combined inn and saloon.

They hadn't stepped three feet into the crowded, smoky room when they were assaulted with a sight they had assumed they wouldn't see until the next day.

As all eyes turned toward the brothers walking into the loud room, the music that had been playing from the corner piano came to a stop, and the sounds of clinking glasses and laughing conversation all ceased.

And four uniformed Union soldiers, with long rifles held in tight grips, rushed the brothers from both sides of the room.

As the Malloy brothers were thrown to the dirty, sawdust-covered floor, their bags stripped away from them and their defenses held at bay by rough hands holding them down, a voice from the past boomed across the room.

A pit of despair opened in the stomachs of both brothers and they simultaneously began to hatch plans to get away, but the voice brought them back to the present, and the dire situation into which they had walked.

"Well, well," the voice, used to command and control, boomed loudly. "I guess I finally got the better of the infamous Malloy brothers."

Gavin and Colt had time to look up and sneer as General Ulysses Harrison, Leader of the Pennsylvania Regulars, and Vice-Command of the Army of the North, limped over to the brothers now being practically sat on by Union infantry.

"I've been waiting a whole week to see you, Gavin Malloy, just like this. A fish flopping on the deck, trussed up like a pig, set for supper."

The general squatted down, belying his age and infirmity, grimacing in a painful way at the two young men lying prone on the dirty floor.

But there was no smile in the general's words, and the Malloy brothers felt the proverbial noose tighten slowly, inexorably, around their very necks.

Chapter 5

The General sighed greatly, kneeling down just in front of the brothers' heads. Silence still permeated the room, and no one seemed to move, nor breathe.

"I need your help, Gavin Malloy."

Shock registered through the bodies of both brothers at the general's words. Gavin looked up with mistrust as the general commanded the infantrymen to pick the brothers up off the floor.

Colt stretched his shoulders back as they watched the general limp back to a corner table, his own shoulders sinking down in what could only be described as defeat.

"What the hell," Gavin muttered to his brother.

Colt only shook his head, not uttering a word. But Gavin knew his brother's mind better than anyone. Colt was as shocked as he was, and the bigger shock was that Colt wouldn't have to fight his way free.

Gavin knew that his brother's body was terribly shook at the sudden drop of rage, loss of adrenaline and the buildup in both their bodies for the fighting.

But neither Malloy had time to register all that was happening. The infantrymen behind them, rifles still held at the ready, pushed both brothers in the back toward where the general was sitting, nursing a whiskey glass, his head hung low over the scarred table.

Two other chairs faced the general, and the brothers knew those chairs were for them.

As they sat down at the table, warily watching the general for any movement or an inkling of understanding of what was going on, the noise and bustle sounded loudly around them once more.

The silence at their small table soon grew uncomfortable, however, and as Gavin was about to ask the general just what the hell they were doing there, and why the two brothers weren't already swinging from the deadly end of a noose, the old man looked up at the two of them, tears glimmering in his bloodshot eyes.

The general took a deep breath, settled his emotions, and placed both hands flat on the table between the men. Gavin noticed that the general's fingernails were bitten down almost to the quick, and small, bloody troughs existed where hangnails once were.

Not a good sign of the general's mental state, he thought to himself right before the man started speaking in a bold, tense voice.

"Gavin, my daughter, Rye, was kidnapped from her room, right under my nose, two weeks ago," he said all in one breath.

Both Malloy brothers were taken aback. That sure as hell wasn't what they thought there were going to hear.

"I offer both of you a pardon for your crimes against the Union Army, five full years pay, and a stipend for the duration of the job I have for you," the general said.

Gavin wanted to talk, to ask a million questions, but Colt gently laid his hand on his little brother's arm, silencing him. One look at Colt, and Gavin knew they needed to hear the rest of the offer, and what exactly the job was.

"Gavin, you are the damn finest manhunter I've ever heard of. I knew that if anyone could find the bastards that took my baby, it would be you." The general's eyes started to tear up again.

"If you find my daughter, or her body, and get rid of the men who did this, in the most… ahh… imaginative way you can think of, I'll make sure you both receive your pardons and bounties," he finally finished.

"And we all know just how imaginative the two of you can be, don't we?" he asked both younger men.

The brothers swallowed hard at the old man's words, and the barrage of memories the words brought to both brothers' minds.

Like a few days before hand, the sounds of gunfire, loud in their ears, hot blood splattering and pooling, and bodies laying prone in dirty roads tried to take over both minds and souls.

But all that made Gavin think of one other thing. A thought that might help the brothers keep from hanging from that noose by morning.

The veteran officer, and extremely experienced general, used to commanding thousands of men, sometimes tens of thousands during the bloody height of the War, and marshalling whole battlefields, was at a loss.

He would never have come to the Malloy's if he wasn't.

Strategy and execution may have been the general's strongest suits, but he couldn't begin to imagine how to find his own daughter, or how to start down the trails of finding single individuals hiding in the largest unoccupied frontier in the world, which the Brothers Malloy just so happened to excel at.

And that gave the brothers a huge advantage over the man they had both come to hate since leaving the Army years before.

Looking at each other, the general waiting impatiently for their answers, the brothers knew only a single fact beyond anything the general said.

If they didn't help the man, they would be strung up on the desertion charges that very day and be hanging from a tree branch before the sun rose the next morning.

The general didn't have to tell them those facts. They could hear it between the words of anguish the older man spoke.

And they both knew that no matter how long it took, they had better damned well succeed at the task. If for any reason they didn't, the general would exact revenge on the brothers and not the kidnappers.

The Brothers Malloy suddenly found themselves between the proverbial rock and hard place. They both knew they had been securely defeated even before the battle started.

The general was no idiot.

And the worst part was, Gavin thought to himself as he looked into the embattled, yet still bright eyes of their former commanding officer, *the old codger knew it better than both of them at that moment.*

Gavin sighed deeply, reached over to take the half-full glass of strong whiskey sitting between the general's hands, and drank the contents in a single, stinging gulp.

"Better tell me everything," he said to the old man, grimacing at both the sting of the harsh whiskey and the harsher reality of what lay before them all.

Chapter 6

"I didn't hear anything at all that night." The general was practically sobbing into his new glass of whiskey.

Gavin watched as the soldiers around the room settled down with their own glasses or moved outside to take up post.

He went back to listening intently to the general's story. Anything could be the key to finding Rye Harrison. And anything, if missed, could end up the death of the last of the line of Malloy's.

"When I went up the next morning to get her up for breakfast, which I have to do sometimes, she likes to sleep in sometime, you see," General Harrison went on.

"Her bed had not been slept in, and she was nowhere to be found." The general sobbed loudly.

He took a long swallow of the strong whiskey in his almost empty glass.

"I had most of the help looking for her on the grounds all that morning," he told the two brothers.

"But all that was found were her bed slippers near the west end of the grounds, and not a hair else."

And with that, the general finally let his military bearing founder, and full, loud tears fell from his bloodshot eyes.

"Bring my baby home to me, Gavin Malloy," the general gasped through his sobs.

Gavin actually felt for the old man in that moment.

"Bring her home to me, and I'll give you anything. She's all I have left of her mother." The general's words faded into a whisper with that last line, but both men heard him.

They'd had no idea that the General had a wife and had barely remembered that he had a daughter.

To both brothers, through four years of bloody war and death on all sides, the man sitting forlornly in front of them, sobbing into his whiskey glass, had been a pillar of military might, stoic and like a wall when he gave the command to put other men to death.

This man in front of them, with emotions leaking from his very soul and out of his eyes, was not the tough piece of hickory the brothers had known previously.

The difference was jarring in both men's minds.

Soon, the brothers stood up, leaving the general asleep, spent emotionally, and snoring in his cups. The other Army officer with the small attachment of infantrymen didn't hinder or stop the two from heading up to the bar and inquiring of the innkeeper for a room and a bath.

Within an hour, both of the Malloy brothers were enjoying hot baths, clean towels, and the knowledge that while their futures weren't promised, and they had no idea where to start on their journey, at least this day they were taken care of, comfortable, and their horses and belongings stowed and settled.

They would figure out where to start the next day.

And Gavin, at least, hoped they found the young woman quickly, took care of the men who would do such a dastardly deed, and returned home to a ranch still theirs for the calling.

Colt Malloy, however, didn't care one way or another.

He knew more than anyone that even if they found the woman, it didn't mean that the general wouldn't still act out what he had promised the two men years before.

Years earlier, after Colt had punched the general square in the face for his denial of dismissal for the two brothers at the conclusion of the War, after they had both high-tailed it out of the military headquarters in Washington D.C., he could still hear the screams of the old man.

"I don't care if it's the last thing I do on God's green earth, Malloy's," the general had shouted at the fleeing men.

"I will see you both hanging from a tree for what you've done!"

Colt Malloy, sitting warm and comfortable in the large iron tub in the middle of his room at the inn, could still feel the shivers he had felt, knowing that he could take a bullet in the back at any moment as he had fled the military outpost.

He didn't for a moment trust that the general wouldn't use the brothers like he had done all through the War, and then get rid of them once they had served their purposes, just like he had done over and over and over again.

His chills soon turned the warm water tepid.

And then the familiar body shakes started once again, only assuaged with the bottle of whiskey he had grabbed from the barkeep downstairs, knowing he needed to be lost to the memories in order to sleep, once again.

Chapter 7

"I don't think that we will both be able to head back to the ranch, Colt," Gavin told his brother over breakfast the next morning.

"I can get the general to supply us here, probably buy a pack horse." Gavin paused, deep in thought, his eggs and bacon forgotten in front of him.

Colt got his attention again when he reached across the small table and speared one of Gavin's strips of almost-burned bacon from his plate.

"Right," Gavin said. "Go to the post office. See if a rider heading north can get a letter to Porter. We are going to need Heath, and probably one of the cattle boys."

His mind was going a mile a minute.

"Write Porter and send him up to the camps. Get Heath and his Army buddy, what was his name?" Gavin asked his brother, forkful of scrambled eggs halfway to his mouth. Colt answered his question around loudly chewing his own bacon.

"Russ. Russ O'Shanashay."

"Right," Gavin said again. "Him and Heath should be enough. We need to travel light and quick."

"Ahh, hell, Colt, forget the letter. Just better go yourself and do all that. Don't know how long it'll take, but we need to get on the trail soon as can be, most like."

Gavin's mind wasn't as sharp and organized as it had been in the past, but it was coming back slowly.

"You better head back to the ranch and get our guns, ammo, the long-winter packs, and anything else you know we will need. You've done this before, big brother."

Colt suddenly cleared his throat loudly.

Looking up and behind Gavin, his eyes then fell to meet his brother's and Gavin knew one of the officers, if not the general himself, had entered the small eating room off of the inn's main saloon area.

A large hand fell heavily on Gavin's shoulder, and it took everything he had to not draw on whoever had invaded his personal space and ruin everything right then and there.

"Boys, General wants you in his drawing room, if you please," the nasally voice of the general's aide-de-camp sounded behind Gavin's head.

"Be right up," Gavin answered, shrugging the meaty hand off of his shoulder.

"*Now*, gentlemen, if you don't mind," Lt. General Walter Mondaulk said, exasperated.

"Damn it, Walter, we'll be up when we finish breakfast." Gavin wasn't going to give the older boot-licker any more respect than he shoveled back at the brothers. Gavin's hip still ached where he had hit it on the hard wooden floor the day before. No thanks to Walter Mondaulk.

"I'll inform General Harrison then," the older man said with a sniff.

As the career infantryman left in a huff behind him, leaving out the same door behind Gavin that he had entered, Colt rolled his eyes.

"Never did like that guy," he said.

Gavin just nodded his head in agreement. They had more to discuss and prepare, and Gavin wanted his best friend and riding companion hot on the trail south before the week was out.

"Colt, I'll go up and lick the general's boots, see if we can't get outfitted properly. You go get to Porter and get those boys headed this way by weeks' end," Gavin instructed.

When it came to being on the hunt, Colt deferred to his little brother every time. Gavin had a skillset that most men didn't, and Colt respected the man enough to know Gavin knew what he was doing.

The two brothers finished scraping their plates clean hurriedly and drank the last of the black coffee in the tin mugs the innkeeper's daughter had supplied.

As they pushed back their chairs from the breakfast table, Colt looked one last time at his little brother, and what had been on both men's minds slipped out of his mouth.

"You sure we can find the girl, little brother?" he asked Gavin.

"Hell, Colt, I ain't sure of anything. I just know we're dead if we don't try," Gavin answered.

Before they left the comfortably-appointed breakfast room, Gavin said one last thing over his shoulder that made Colt's spine shiver in fear.

"But I'd rather take my chances on the trail than sitting here hoping the general's changed his mind on stringing us up for not staying in the Army when the War ended, no matter what the old codger says," he told Colt in parting.

Gavin watched his brother grab his hat and head out the door, heading back home before he, himself, headed up the stairs to the grand rooms at the upper front end of the Inn. Colt knew the way north and home, and Gavin wondered distractedly if he, himself, would ever see home again.

And he knew that Colt would be thinking the same on the way north.

Getting to the top of the stairs, he figured he knew where the general was supposed to be, and that the general's rooms would be the grandest in the establishment.

No doubt very few notable and heroic Civil War heroes came through these parts, he thought as he hastily made his way up the old grand stairway.

Better not keep the old coot waiting long.

He walked to the front of the inn using the long upper hallway at the top of the stairs, and soon saw the same two infantrymen standing guard at the door that had ambushed the brothers the day before.

"Gentlemen," Gavin greeted as he moved between them and opened the door to the general's drawing room.

The two soldiers' barely held-in contempt for the man they had heard so many stories about was worn plain on their faces. Gavin Malloy had been a hero in his own right, right up until he and his brother had deserted at the drawing down of the war.

Gavin didn't give one lick what the lowly soldiers thought of him. He knew the full story of what had transpired in that office in D.C. that day, and he couldn't care less what rumors and wild tales went around the camps about the Malloy brothers' escape from Washington D.C.

Gavin walked into the richly appointed drawing room, noticing the fine artwork on the walls, the heavy wooden furniture scattered around the medium-sized room, and the stuffiness of too many bodies pressed too close together around the single desk and chair in the middle of the area.

As Gavin cleared his throat loudly, a space was made by the soldiers standing around the desk, and Gavin could see the old man himself, holding court like a king of old.

General Ulysses Harrison was wearing his golden tassels and had leaned his famous Army-issued rapier against the desk next to him.

A pure white, wide-brimmed officer's hat with golden plumage sat resolutely next to the old man, who was glancing at a stack of maps before him.

Gavin had seen this same scene enough times during the war to know that the war was not over for these men.

Probably never will be, he thought to himself as he walked toward the desk where the general was beckoning him over.

"Before we get into the other matter, Malloy," the General said to him as he walked to the front end of the desk, moving several officers out of the way.

"What can you tell me about the Blackfeet incursions around these parts?"

So, the general wasn't just in Montana Territory to get the aid of the Malloy brothers to find his daughter. *All work*, Gavin thought as he rolled his eyes.

The general was killing two birds with one stone, and that was just like the man.

"Can't tell you much more than they harass decent ranch folks and scatter livestock for fun," Gavin told the old man in barely held-in impatience.

"Can you tell me where they camp? Where the villages or what passes for them in these parts are located on this here map?" the general asked.

"Nope, General. They move around a lot. Never in the same spot twice," he told the old man.

The general just nodded. He moved the top map, which Gavin could tell was a detailed rendering of the very Territory that the boys had grown up in, and in which they were major land holders now, off the desk resolutely.

Seeing the details of the map gave Gavin pause. He had not known that the Army had such knowledge of the whole of the frontier around them.

"Let's talk about what we know about my daughter's kidnapping then," the general said.

Gavin heard a small catch in the man's voice.

Well, not completely without a soul, Gavin thought as he perked up his ears to hear the tale. Any little clue would help him know where to start.

"So, as I told you boys yesterday, there was no trace of my Rye, except her slippers," the general was saying.

"There were no clothes taken from her rooms, and even her bed had been made, even though I know she had gone to bed. I looked in on her as I usually do, before I went to my own bed," he told Gavin.

Gavin itched to ask more questions, but he let the old man go on to see if any clues popped out at him.

"We checked her jewelry, makeup drawer, even her diary," General Harrison said, looking down at the desk in front of him.

"There was nothing out of place, and nothing that stood out, except her absence and the slippers at the end of the property."

Gavin finally had to ask a question that had been itching his mind the entire time since he had learned of the kidnapping.

"Sir, the slippers. Where were they found, and was there anything odd by their location?" he asked the older man.

"Well, no. They were pointing east, out away from my land. And other than the dead snake next to them, nothing would stand out as odd," he told the younger Malloy.

"Wait, sir, wait," Gavin butted in.

"What dead snake?" he asked, excitedly.

"Just some dead snake son, we have them all the time in the summer. It's hot as a witch's tit in church where I have lands," he told Gavin, getting slightly annoyed.

"Yes, but sir, what kind of snake was it?" Gavin was feeling the old, familiar feeling of being on the precipice of learning where to start the hunt.

"Well, now that you ask that, it is a bit odd," the general said, his annoyance slipping away like butter on a hot iron pan.

Gavin felt goosebumps up and down his spine. He knew what the general was going to say before he even said it.

"I had only ever seen them out east. Those red, black, and yellow coral snakes," the general said.

And then ideas like bright lights went off in Gavin's head.

He knew right where he and Colt and the boys needed to go, and they had better move fast.

"Shit," was all Gavin could mutter under his breath.

He almost bolted from the general's rooms, but the next words out of the old man's mouth stopped him short.

"You know who did this, don't you, Malloy?" the general asked.

Gavin didn't want to lie to the general, but he also knew that the Army had no chance of finding the young woman.

There weren't more than three or four people who knew where to look, and who to talk to, to find the person who would leave a deadly, out-of-place, eastern coral snake at the scene of a kidnapping.

The only person Gavin had ever known who dealt in deadly snakes, alive and dead.

"Yes, sir, I do," Gavin told him. "And you better equip me and my brother quick. If I'm right, your daughter is in more danger than you know."

Silence filled the room suddenly. The tension was palpable.

And as the general stood up, pushing the chair he had been sitting in back roughly, and giving the younger Malloy brother a stare that could curdle milk, you could hear a pin drop like a hammer falling on an anvil.

"And who, pray-tell, stole my little girl from her very bed?" the general asked in the most menacing voice Gavin had ever heard.

The general's eyes were squinting, his body quivering in rage, and Gavin could feel the anxiety in the postures and sudden stiff backs of the men surrounding him.

He knew that not only his life, but a risk of the entire country burning, was the stake he risked with the truthfulness of his next words.

He cleared his throat loudly, and said a name as honestly as he could, knowing the people in the room would not know of whom he spoke.

"Snakebite McGee, sir. And I'm the only man alive who can find the old witch."

Gavin suddenly felt the other boot fall, and chill bumps stood out on all the exposed skin of his body, making his spine pucker up and start to shake.

Chapter 8

The rest of that week was a slow hell for Gavin.

The only redeeming quality was that halfway through it, on Wednesday, the general and his cohorts moved out of the small town and headed off into the wild Montana Territory to put down the Blackfeet uprising.

Gavin realized, with the general's last dire warning, just how wrong he and his brother had figured things from the simple letter that had started this whole damn ordeal.

"Listen, boy, you find my daughter alive, you bring her home, no matter what it costs you," the general had told him from horseback out front of the inn the morning the Army headed north and east.

"Bring her home to me, in Oregon, to her home, or I'll burn everything and everyone you've ever known to the ground, so help me God."

Gavin had simply nodded, holding the bills of tender from the Army Supply Depot, bills that would supply him and his brother and anyone they had with them for the duration of finding Rye Harrison and getting her back to her home in Oregon.

The rest of the week, leading into the weekend, Gavin simply waited for his brother and the two men who should be accompanying him.

Gavin knew it would take some time for the men to get to the ranch from the gold rush camps deep in the mountains north of the Malloy land.

But that sure didn't make waiting any easier.

Gavin's entire body was taut as a bowstring, and the slightest movements and sounds burned his nerve endings.

By the end of the week, he was like to pop from impatience.

But the three men rode into town around noon on Saturday, and Gavin wanted to hug his brother's neck just for relieving his tension and boredom.

Gavin hugged his best friend, Heath, as the man alit from his dappled mare, and he shook hands with both his brother and Russ. He turned back, clapped Heath loudly on the shoulder, and ushered the three men into the dusky saloon for drinks and entertainment before heading out the next day.

He needed to give them the plans and the rundown on all he had learned since waiting for the trio to show.

Soon enough, the four men sat down with drinks, loud, raucous conversations and games of poker taking place around the group.

He gave Colt, Heath, and the red headed Irish lad, Russ O'Shanashay, whom the brothers had met on a few occasions, the rundown on where they were starting, and which direction they were going to travel, as they sat around a poker table for most of the rest of that afternoon.

Seeing Heath Kirkeby for the first time in many months brought joy to Gavin's heart in ways he couldn't explain. The man had been his closest friend, besides his brother Colt, for more years than he could count. And count on the man, he did. Often.

Heath had his own experiences in the War that he didn't discuss much, and the Malloy brothers didn't push. But get him in the whiskey, and around a bright campfire on a dark, cloudless night, and he would relay some of the more gruesome things he had seen and done in the four years of fighting.

"I only know of one man that would know where Snakebite would be holed up, and that's Archer, down there in Tascosa," Gavin said.

"He's like a father to the old witch, and if anyone knows why she would kidnap someone like Rye Harrison, and where she would stash her, it would be Archer," Gavin finished telling the three other men sitting around him, drinking beers and whiskey.

"We head down to Texas, see Archer at Old Churchman's Crossing, and we should know where to go after that," Gavin finished.

"A dead snake, and one old man out of everyone in the nation, brother?" Colt asked.

"Not a lot to go on," he finished.

"I've gone on less, Colt, and you know it," Gavin replied.

Colt just shrugged his affirmation. He had trusted his little brother with less information than this before. And he would do it again.

Russ, the young Irishman, finally spoke up.

"Heath said there'd be a bounty. What ya' figger the Army gonna pay us?" he asked Gavin.

"Well, whatever it is, you and Heath will be splitting it. Me and Colt feel grateful just to get the Army off our backs and allowing us to get back to life on the ranch without looking over our shoulders," Gavin said, taking a long swallow of warming beer.

Colt, once again, just nodded his affirmation.

"Alright then, boys. When are we getting started?" Heath asked the table.

All eyes turned to Gavin. He would be the trail boss on this excursion, as always.

"Tomorrow. It'll take a week to get to Tascosa, and from there, who knows where we're headed," he said.

Everyone around the table just nodded their heads, finished drinks, and went about finding entertainment and comfort before hitting the trail the next day.

Colt ushered Gavin over to a corner where there was a modicum of silence so he could whisper in Gavin's ear.

"I don't like this, little brother," he whispered, knowing no one could hear him. But he had to say what was on his mind anyway.

"We don't know what'll happen to us once we return the girl," he finished.

His eyes looked serious, and Gavin had never seen his brother so shaken since the War.

"We will figure it out like we always do, big brother," Gavin tried to assure Colt. But the same thoughts had been racing through Gavin's mind as well over the last week.

The country was getting to be a ridiculously small place, he knew, and it was getting increasingly difficult for two men to hide in a rapidly shrinking frontier.

But they had more at stake than just their lives. They had the ranch, and people who depended on the two of them.

Gavin wasn't ready to stop living just yet, and he would do whatever he could to protect his brother, his property, and the legacy they both wanted to eventually leave to children, should God bless them in that way.

But they had a past they would have to face, and serious sins they would have to answer for, he knew.

He just prayed and hoped an answer would come before the end of the manhunt they were about to set out on.

He prayed a miracle would keep his and his brother's necks out of the ropes long enough to live the good lives they had always wanted, and had worked against with almost zero choice, since they were old enough to shoot pistols.

He knew Colt felt the same way, and after clapping his brother soundly on the shoulder and moving off to find a way to distract himself from the dark thoughts floating through his mind, that prayer and wish never quite went away.

They set out the next morning before the sun arose in the east, with resolute hearts, sound minds, sturdy backs, and four gun-callused hands ready to take care of anything that came between them and returning the kidnapped young woman back to her father.

    Come hell or high water, Gavin thought to himself as they rode south at a fast clip and watched the rising dawn brighten to their left, *they would succeed, or die trying.*

Part 2
A Hot and Evil Wind Blows Up From the South

Chapter 9

The year after the War of the North and the South, now known as the Civil War, ended, the demand for good beef in the northwestern states rose high enough to change age-old habits and ways of life.

The need for money in one area of the world that had plenty of beef, and the need for beef in another area that was rich in cash, but low in good meat, was the perfect handshake for new, innovative approaches to answer economic issues.

It was the old supply and demand that drove desperate men to do brave, new things, and put money and resources into the pockets of men just like them, and at the same time, put food on the tables of families around the nation.

It was how progress was made, but it usually had to have a catalyst, and that was a man or woman with a new plan, and a new way of doing things.

And that was exactly the problem facing the hungry gold rush camps and small towns growing to large cities throughout the north and west in those years following the War.

The question was how to get the beef from deep in the hot, southern climes, up to the north, where cold and lack of year-round grasses had kept cattle ranches from popping up like the gold rush camps.

And the issue needed figgerin' out, so to say.

And a young, intrepid miner, who had struck it rich in those same gold rush camps in the north was who finally did the figgerin'.

A smart and driven man named Nelson Story used his profits from the gold fields of Alder Gulch, Montana Territory, to purchase one thousand longhorns in Texas the year after the War ended.

Nelson himself was a bit of a local legend. He had always had a head for figgerin' out problems, and if anyone were going to find gold in Alder Gulch, it'd be him, locals always said.

He and his beautiful bride, Ellen Trent Story, began working the field that everyone else had passed off as 'full of grit, gravel, some ash, but not a lick of gold,' and within a few months had amassed a staggering $30,000 in gold dust.

But Story wasn't happy with just some gold dust. He was a visionary, an orphan, a vigilante from the War, and had worked as a freight driver out of Colorado before meeting his industrious wife.

So, he traded his $30,000 in gold dust for $20,000 in cash and headed south.

He and Ellen had devised a daring, bold plan.

Arriving at the famous Fort Worth Stockyards, Story and his lovely bride soon purchased some one thousand head of cattle, Texas Longhorns to be exact, for half his cash reserves.

He had got them cheap, as the economy all through the South was devastated after the long, bloody war.

Nelson Story wasn't the only man with the same plan, but he was definitely the first man with enough resources to do what came next the right way.

The summer of 1866 saw some 260,000 head of cattle, bought cheap on the Texas High Plains, driven north to the gold rush camps all throughout the northwestern United States.

And Nelson Story was at the head of all that trail ridin', cattle drivin', money makin' economic recovery.

The 1866 cattle drives were not without their fair share of trouble, however.

Jayhawkers from Kansas, cattle robbers, Indians in Oklahoma who had survived the Trail of Tears, and at every town and crossing, fees assessed per head of cattle, made the drive impossible for most.

But not for the dogged and determined Story and his beautiful bride, Ellen.

With a large measure of courage, and even larger share of luck, Nelson Story and his wife drove their herd of over one thousand head of Texas Longhorns up the newly named Bozeman trail, blazing a way for future cattle drives to make it to the bustling and growing Bozeman, Montana.

Story and his cowboys were hampered by the US Army, the Sioux uprising lead by legendary Chief Red Cloud, along with fees, weather, sickness, and the loss of a single cowboy to Sioux arrows.

But for the first time in US history, a cattle drive of that size and magnitude survived the harrowing straits and troubles on the frontier trails, and arrived, successfully, in Bozeman, five months and two thousand miles from where they had set out from in Texas.

The feat wouldn't be duplicated again for another four years, but that drive made Nelson Story the first millionaire in the Montana Territory, and a legend in his own right.

And it was that same trail, down the Bozeman markers, that four young cowboys found themselves on, a few years later.

The Malloy brothers told the tale of their friend and mentor, Nelson Story, to the rapt attention of their best friend Heath, and his work companion, Russ, on the quick ride south.

They were headed to the Texas panhandle three years after that first, famous cattle drive, and many of the hazards and perils that Nelson had faced weren't a factor any longer.

But that didn't mean that the trail south wouldn't still have its own pitfalls and troubles.

So, as the group of young men rode south at as fast a clip as they dared to risk, they kept a keen eye out for trouble, and set a watch through the nights, when the land was darkest, and the highest risk of raid or murder abounded.

The Malloy brothers had been on these same trails more times than they liked to remember, but Heath and Russ were wet-behind-the-ears rookies on long trail rides, and so Gavin took it upon himself to ease the men's minds by retelling stories of things that had happened to him and Colt during the War, and showed the men how they had got through some harrowing situations without a scratch.

It was just imperative to keep their wits about them, their guns well maintained, and their reflexes honed and lightning quick.

And so, besides telling the men stories from past manhunts, they practiced quick drawing and target practice each evening when they stopped to rest and water the horses.

Colt took up his customary job of cook, and pans of cowboy stew, old SOS, and bootheel coffee were regular fare around the campfires late into the nights.

It was a nice, familiar time for the Malloy brothers, and soon, the other two members of their small posse were comfortable as well.

Laughter and general ribbing accompanied each evening's practice, and stories and jokes went between the riders during the long, hot days on the trail south, looking for water each day, and a spot to camp each night.

It was going so well, it was easy for the Malloy brothers to forget what there were doing, how their lives hung in the balance, and the question of why the Harrison girl was kidnapped at all.

But as they moved south toward Oklahoma Territory, and the home of the Five Nations, events transpired quickly to bring the men back to the task at hand, with all the comfort and joy far behind them, and only hardship, blood, and death before them.

For the War wasn't over for many men in the South, and losing the war sure didn't sit well to men who had known only years of death, loss, and blood.

Gangs of southern Confederate marauders and cattle thieves sprung up like weeds, and as desperation and hunger drove them to commit atrocities normally reserved for the deranged and psychopathic, men like the Malloy brothers and their friends soon learned that they would have to sink to the same levels to not only survive, but to survive long enough to see their mission and task complete.

And to save the life of a young woman they didn't even know was alive, who might already be dead, rotting in a shallow grave, somewhere between Oregon and the only place they knew to look for old Snakebite McGee.

Old Churchman's Crossing, at Tascosa, the Wild West outlaw hideout, and the most murderous capital of an outlaw region.

The place was known to be hell bent on raising the Confederacy from the grave, or if not that, then exacting revenge on any good Christian man or woman, who happened to be unlucky enough to cross paths with the desperate and lowest of lows of the criminal South.

But the Malloy brothers, along with their two friends, hadn't even made it that far before they were waylaid one night by a group of rogues with eyes only on killin' and stealin' anything of value from the four unsuspecting men sleeping under a sheltering overhang of clean sandstone, on

the southern fringes of the Oklahoma Territory panhandle, on
a warm, innocent, and full moon Saturday night.

Chapter 10

The idea, when the men had set off from Montana Territory late in the summer, was to head almost dead south through the Wyoming Territory, into the Colorado Rockies on the east side of the range, so as to skirt deadly summer storms in the high reaches, and then head into New Mexico and turn sharply left, on into the Texas panhandle.

But things on the trail never went according to plan, and the men who had survived such narrowing straits were the most flexible and could change course with but a thought.

And so, as a high plains summer storm had arisen a few weeks back, the four men had been forced to head further east than they had wanted to, into Kansas Territory, thus cutting off all hope of making suitable time, or even seeing New Mexico.

But that was still alright.

They were following the cut-through Bozeman trail southward, and something about being on a land strip with markers that had a home back from their own homeland made the boys feel somewhat better.

Especially when heading south to the Public Land Strip of the Oklahoma Territory.

But entering what most called 'No Man's Land' was a frightful proposition.

A proposition that Gavin and Colt discussed in whispers, as the border crept closer and closer. They were camped down for the night, a quarter-day's quick march from the Oklahoma border, and tensions, between the brothers at least, were growing.

There was no choice, really, Colt had told his little brother, as they discussed skirting further west, bypassing the treacherous land altogether.

They were already running out of time. They had been four weeks on the trail south and weren't getting any closer to finding out answers about Ms. Rye Harrison.

So, the next morning, without telling the other two young men in their party about the dangers they all faced, they saddled up on freshly watered and rested horses, and headed south toward the unfriendly land grant.

Assuming they could trot or gallop through the rough land strip, and head down into a somewhat less lawless Texas, was the plan of the day.

But as always, plans hardly ever worked out, especially when the first bullets started flying. It was a mantra that Gavin Malloy, at the least, had lived by for most of his short life.

Midway through the hot, sunny day, as the four cowboys trotted south through the rocky, brush laden land strip, and without a soul in sight, Heath's horse stepped into a hidden gopher hole, and stumbling, threw Heath end over end to land in a patch of sticky cactus.

After laughing it off and assuring the horse didn't pull up lame or suffer a broken leg, the men took a noon-time break for lunch, and laughed while they all took turns pulling long cactus barbs out of Heath's clothing and skin.

The work took longer than they had figured, and by the time Heath was ready to jump back in the saddle and continue south, the day had grown dusky, and overhead clouds obscured the sunset, making the land around them dangerously dark.

They knew not to push further that day. Risking their horse's legs and their own safety riding a dark trail was more worrisome than camping the night through in the No Man's Land Territory.

Or so they had thought as they bedded down without a fire, between a sandstone outcropping and under a bit of overhang, halfway up a short mesa. By now, the other two men were aware of the danger that they were all in, and Heath was busy cursing himself for missing the gopher hole in the tall brambles earlier that day.

Gavin was sure to calm the young man, but Heath still berated himself as they all went through the quiet preparations for a cold dinner and quieting down the horses.

Thank goodness there was a stout wind blowing up from the south, Gavin thought to himself as they set about making camp within the sheltering south side of the short mesa.

They would be sheltered on the southern side of the mesa and would hear anything coming from further forward in the land strip.

There was no tangible way to hide the five horses tethered together, but they could at least get everyone, and the horses, sheltered close together, under the overhang, to afford a modicum of safety.

Which was exactly the very preparations that saved all four men's lives, during the deep witching hours of that dark, windy night.

Old Garvey, and his three cousins, Clem, Hick, and johnny boy crept up on the sleeping cowboys, hellbent on stealin' and killin'.

The ladyfolk were hungry, and complaining ever' day about the clothes getting holey and the kiddos going without.

So, the four men of the Campton Clan, one of the most dangerous families living in the many abandoned homesteads of the area, snuck up on the cowpokes, not too much care in the world.

If they had known who they were sneaking up on, they would have gone home and tried it with less easy prey later on. But the Campton Clan sure weren't the brightest bunch in 'no-man's land.'

It was not the bullet ricocheting off the sandstone outcropping directly over the men's heads that woke up Gavin from a fitful sleep.

It was the spray of gravel and sand that hit him square in the face that did the trick.

He, along with his brother Colt, were instantly on their feet, pistols held firmly in hand.

"Why would they shoot first?" Colt whispered too loudly to Gavin.

The younger Malloy brother only shook his head and gruffly kicked awake the other two men, still sleeping in bedrolls pulled close together.

"That was one pistol round," Gavin whispered back, ducking behind the short boulders dotting the sloping side of the mesa and looking down into the flat land where the shot had come from.

"It ain't Indians, or professionals," he finished.

Colt just nodded his agreement.

The other two men, finally awake and not real sure what was going on, were hastily ducking down near Gavin, ready to do what the trained and experienced man told them to do.

And rubbing sleep from their eyes while they did it.

The Malloy brothers, on the other hand, were wide awake and ready to rain down hellfire on anyone below.

All four men had weapons in their hands. The Malloy brothers and Heath carried their pistols, while Russ had grabbed the Henry Rifle he had bedded down with.

Luckily, the four men, along with their horses, were sheltered enough and had enough high ground to assure safety.

Because after a muffled shout from down below the south-facing, heavily-brushed mesa slope, all hell suddenly broke loose.

"Idiots," was all Gavin Malloy said as the bullets hit and missed all around the small group.

And with that, and the bullets flying around them harmlessly, Gavin heard something he thought he would never hear again.

His older brother, Colt Malloy, laughing uproariously, and out loud.

The sound shocked Gavin more than the bullets flying harmlessly around the group.

And it had the sudden effect of making the other men feel comfortable and laugh along with the generally stoic man.

A sense of insane festivity pervaded the four men, as with the temporary ceasing of fire from the inexperienced bandits below the mesa, it caused them all to arise from their sheltered spot simultaneously, and run, laughing still, toward the five or six ragged and starving men on foot, crouched themselves in a small grove of rocky boulders at the foot of the small mesa.

It was all over within a few seconds, with six skin-and-bone, dirty, and obviously starving bandits lying dead and splayed at the feet of the four cowboys.

The deaths of the starving men sobered up the group, and the laughter ceased immediately.

But for a while, for the six now deceased outlaws at least, it must have seemed like Hell itself had come barreling down the hillside, demonic laughter following behind a rain of a much more precise storm of bullets than their own had been.

And as Russ loudly retched and threw up his dinner a few feet away, and Heath's face took on a paler countenance in the moonlight, Gavin and Colt Malloy simply nodded to each other, and knew there would be no more sleep that night.

"We'll leave the bodies for the vultures and anyone thinking of following us further," Gavin said, holstering his six-shooter cleanly.

With that, they saddled up in the pre-dawn light from the east and headed toward destiny and hopeful answers.

Chapter 11

"I've been through these parts four different times looking for inscription dodgers and turncoats," Gavin told the group.

They were hunkered down within a deep, dry gully that crisscrossed the mesquite-covered landscape in north Texas, and he wanted to express the severity of danger to the two men who had never been through the outlaw Texas panhandle.

"And every time, I almost lost my life, or at the very least, a body part," he finished with a smile.

The two inexperienced cowpokes on either side of him gulped loudly.

Colt just smiled at his little brother in return.

He remembered his own run-in with Club-foot Mary, a rough-around-the-edges prostitute and renowned bandit in her own right.

It was the last time the brothers had come through the bustling and growing oil town of Amarillo, miles to the south.

He had almost lost a specific body part to the she-demon himself. It was almost a rite of passage for young soldiers.

His smile deepened as he remembered running, once again, for his very life, from a half-naked Club-foot Mary, her brandishing a silver pistol and chasing him down Polk Street for not tipping her more for a mediocre tussle he had enjoyed, drunk and laughing.

The funny, yet sobering memories brought Colt and Gavin both back to the task at hand. The good memories were few and far between, but they sparkled in both men's minds like 4th of July fireworks.

The group was crouched down within yards of the barbed wire fence demarking the lands of the famous XIT Ranch.

And Gavin, at least, didn't feel like getting killed being mistaken for cattle rustlers.

They needed to find the road south and find it fast.

Gavin could almost feel rifle sights being drawn on him from afar. The cowpokes of the XIT Ranch had well-established and well-earned reputations of shooting first and asking questions afterward.

Gavin turned to the other men in his small posse and sighed heavily. There was nothing for it.

He turned onto his back and pulled his wide-brimmed cowboy hat down over his eyes to block out the glaring sunlight.

Folding his hands over his stomach and scootching his backside deeper into the soft sand in the gully, he sighed again.

He knew the other men were just staring at him in bewilderment.

"Might as get a little shut-eye, boys. We can't travel any further south till nightfall," he told them.

He knew that the rustlers and the cowpokes of the XIT took very little care for the barbed-wire-fenced boundaries of the Farwell Brothers' land and would shoot anyone approaching the largest cattle ranch in the world.

Especially anyone coming cross-country from the Land Strip to the north without using the well-known road further to the west.

It was that heavily traveled road south toward Tascosa that they would have to find come dark.

Shouldn't be too hard, Gavin thought to himself as he heard the other men settle into the soft sand of the deep gully.

All they had to do was head west by the stars, with the bright moonlight leading the way.

He dozed most of the afternoon away, comfortably ensconced in the deep gully, out of sight of rifles and trigger-happy cowboys, and enjoying the quiet of the West Texas breeze through the mesquite brush surrounding them in heavy swarths all the way down to Central Mexico.

He was thinking about the first time he had heard the story of how mesquite trees had found their way all the way into the central US when they were not native to this land.

It was the same man they sought in Old Tascosa who had told a much younger Gavin Malloy the tale, while sitting on the deep, rickety front porch of the Old Churchman's Crossing.

Gavin remembered the tale well. As well as the man who told it.

Archer Wisdom. The old prospector-turned-revival preacher himself.

Archer Wisdom had told him that the mesquite seeds were carried and planted from deep within the hooves of the very first beef cattle driven up from central Mexico, decades before, when this land had been ruled and controlled by first Spain and then Mexico.

The mesquite surrounding them, dotting the low desert landscape like sprouts of hair left on an old man's head, had taken to the red and brown dirt of West Texas, and had sprouted like the proverbial weed.

Gavin was enjoying the warmth, and the deepening dusk of the afternoon once the glare of the sun overhead was gone from the shade of his hat still pulled low.

And he was feeling rather good about the rest of the trail south to Old Tascosa.

He didn't think that he would end up shot or hung, and he was fairly certain he could get the rest of his men through the dangerously wild Texas landscape around them.

He was looking forward to a warm bed, a nice bath, some tasty food, and seeing his old friend, Archer Wisdom, in Old Tascosa.

Hell, he thought. *This was feeling almost too easy.*

That was until the first fat, heavy raindrops hit him square on the nose as he moved his hat to see what the sudden commotion around him was all about.

Chapter 12

Some weather could turn a good man downright unruly, Gavin Malloy thought. But other weather, it could downright kill a man, too.

The torrential downpour affecting sight, sound, and footing that was deluging the four men looking for a wide road south was one of the latter kinds, he knew.

And that sure soured the mood he'd had all afternoon lying in the nice warm sun.

The fear of a bullet between the shoulder blades all day had now turned into a fear of weathering the sudden summer storm that had moved swiftly in while the men had snoozed.

And the overwhelming sound of wind and rain was worrying Gavin and Colt both.

As Gavin looked to the sky, seeing the sickly green color of impending doom, as his mother used to always say, he knew the truth most cowboys caught out in the open plains knew.

This was tornado land, and they had to find immediate shelter that wouldn't flood and wash them away with it.

They were stuck between a rock and hard place, and this kind of sudden weather in a dark, stormy night could easily kill a man and wash away all traces.

And then the wind, the rain, the sounds, and the weather around them went suddenly and completely silent.

Not only did the entire world go silent, but the trees dotting the area stood absolutely still, the wind died down completely, and an eerie calm descended from the green sky above that made everything become as surreal as a nightmare you couldn't wake from. The silence lasted what seemed forever but Gavin, at least, knew it was much quicker than that.

The eerie calm lasted for a full five seconds.

The only thing the four men, riding as fast on horseback as they could ride, heard in those five life-threatening seconds was Gavin yelling, and the beat of horse hooves on rock and dirt.

"Shit," he yelled before all hell broke loose.

A sound like the biggest steam-driven train in the world shattered the silence around the men, and all five horses suddenly bucked and almost threw their riders at the onslaught of noise and wind.

It was a twister, and a big one at that, Gavin thought, hanging tightly to the saddle horn below him.

And they were all going to die.

A sudden and bright light to his left brought his head around sharply, and at first, his mind couldn't register what he saw. But his instincts punched in, and he turned old Mabel's head sharply at the sight.

He could feel, but couldn't see, his men follow him toward what was exposed to Gavin in the sudden and blinding blink of several bright lightning bolts.

Mabel lurched unexpectedly, falling the last several feet into a deep, sandstone cave that had erupted on the side of a large hill in the deep canyon-like land they had found themselves in.

He quickly sawed her reins to the left, moving Mabel out of the entrance to the miracle cave, and allowed the rest of the group to crowd in while the storm blew outside.

"What in the actual hell, Gavin?" Colt asked, shaken.

"I don't remember this cave," he finished.

Gavin was equally perplexed at their sudden luck.

And that's when the largest, most terrifying sight any of them had ever seen moved less than a half-mile away through the dark, stormy night.

They could only see the monster twister, gray and terrible in color, through brief, bright flashes of lightning. It had to have been at least a quarter mile wide at the base, and they couldn't see the top of it through the dark storm clouds.

Gavin moved the group further back from the entrance, finding enough room in the cave to shelter them all comfortably.

He, more than they, had seen such a twister before, and knew what it was.

It was death incarnate, and if they had not found the cave they now crowded within, not even moving from atop their mounts, they would have been caught up in the terrible twister, and this trail south would have ended right here and right now.

Gavin could swear he heard maniacal laughter in the terrible and deadly twister outside the shelter they had miraculously found, but he knew it was probably his mind making up greasy ideas as he came down from the sudden and awful rush from seeing their impending death in the flashes of brightest lightning.

Gavin Malloy had no context for, nor had any idea of, how very right his ears were.

He could not see, and could barely hear, as the demons from the dark creation rode the terrible twister, trying to snuff out the Mission currently unfolding and win the very Celestial War that this mission, if successful, could change the tides of.

The entire Host of ArchAngels, both Older and Younger Ilk, as well as hordes of lesser angels of the multitude had been forced to intervene to save the four men below, now safety ensconced in a cave that had not existed five minutes prior. The fighting against the Watchers and the ungodly swarm of dark, twisted things was horrible to behold.

The terrible battle waging within the maelstrom of the oversized twister would have been a nightmarish hellscape to any human watching from below.

The flashes of light from the battles within the Spiritual were so powerfully bright, they escaped into the Material realm, appearing for all intents and purposes as more terrible lightning.

No one alive, Material or Spiritual, had ever before seen anything so powerful that it could transcend the Planes with almost no effort, but at the same time expelling titan quantities of celestial energy.

The four men, safely looking to set up camp in the new cave system, had no real idea how close they had all come to simply being torn from the very existence the Host was trying to save.

They would have had no contextual idea of the resonating consequences for all of Creation, on every plane, if that were to have been allowed.

Inter-Mission 1

The throne room was quiet. Eerily quiet.

Songs of worship and glory, usually a loud and distracting din, had been cut short by the absence of the Father.

Gabriel, the oldest and strongest ArchAngel, stood in the middle of a circle made of the rest of the Host.

He inspected each of his brothers and sisters like a military drill sergeant, looking for hidden weaknesses and lovingly assessing the Host's level of exhaustion and willingness to continue the fight.

He couldn't give strength to the countenances of his brothers and sisters like the Creator could, but he could encourage and support, taking the largest parts of the fighting on himself.

It was a job that he had been doing for all time, space, and creation. And he still didn't mind. Having the aspect of the Creator's love within himself, he would never lose the bottomless supply of hope and love for his fellow ArchAngels.

But the looks on several faces of the Host, and the rents and tears in much of their Heavenly Armor, concerned him. The fighting during this particular Mission was heavier and more taxing than any before.

His golden aura brightening around him, he nodded at several brothers. Giving a strong hand on a sunken shoulder here and there straightened the body of the ArchAngels before him. He had to do that same gesture several times. That was the most concerning part.

It was his brother, the ArchAngel Michael, who finally broke the silence of the bereft throne room. His usual anger and animosity, wrapped in a heart as big as Gabriel's own, showed through the words.

"Where *is* He, Gabriel?" Michael asked, frustrated.

Gabriel looked over at his oldest and dearest brother. He needed to tell them the message that he had been given.

And he knew it would give hope to some, like the Younger Ilk, but to Michael and Raphael, at least, it could spell doom for the War raging outside in the Spiritual realm.

A war that they all still fought, even if parts of their countenances were present here, in the oddly quiet throne room of Heaven.

Gabriel smiled at his brothers and sisters. His Aura brightened until it was almost blinding. He hoped his words would rekindle strength and hope within the Host.

They would need it.

"The Father of All, the Fairest of Ten Thousand, the Morning Star and the Creator of all Existence, has spoken to me," he told the Host.

Several eyes looked up and shoulders lifted in anticipation.

It was never good when the Creator went missing from the Heavens. Not when the entire Host got their very strength and essence from His proximity to them.

"God Himself has told me to tell you to not fear," he went on.

"The Father has decided to take a more… active role in the Mission playing out, in order to assure its completion."

The faces Gabriel had assumed would perk up at the news did just that, while those who were created first, Gabriel amongst them, saw the news for what it was.

A *Doom*, if God wasn't successful.

The thought made a few brightly lit Auras almost shatter in fear.

Gabriel disgustedly hated that part of their angelic makeup.

They had been too closely created like their human siblings for his liking in that regard. Too much emotion for Beings that were supposed to be without fear.

Fear, the *Antithesis* of Faith.

God rarely took a full part in what happened in the Material. And when He had in the past, at least in the Material, whole worlds had been lost, outside of the repeated recycling of those same worlds throughout creation.

A smaller voice spoke up from Gabriel's right. It was his sister, Haniel. Her bluish-white Aura glowed bright with Hope.

"And just how is the Father taking a more pivotal role, Brother?" she asked.

He loved her most. The smallest of them all, Haniel was the favorite of most of the Host. *She must be protected at all costs,* Gabriel thought, not for the first time.

He smiled at her, the deep well of Hope and Faith he enjoyed shared outwardly with his Family.

"Just the way we would think," he said, his smile growing even stronger. "He will be guiding the humans through the next part of their lives, and protecting them Himself. And He is taking His *full* self into it."

That perked up the rest of the Host. They now knew just where God took Himself off to. Smiles radiated around the quiet throne. This Mission had a chance, after all.

How very much like their Father, indeed.

Part 3

Answers Come With a Painful Price

Chapter 13

The rest of the night of the deathly storm was passed in relative quiet and comfort. The cave's sandy floor was soft as a feather mattress, and the small fire that the men were willing to light, in hopes that it wouldn't be seen outside the confines of the magical cave, gave them heat and warm food for the first time in a few days.

The smells of bacon and beans soon permeated the small space, and even the horses seemed to relax and enjoy themselves, feed bags moving in rhythm with their chewing.

As they all bedded down after eating a filling supper, and Gavin Malloy planned the next day's ride along the road they were sure to find early, he allowed himself to relax and sleep deeply for the first time since they had departed Montana Territory weeks earlier.

And as he drifted off to a fitful sleep, and without prompting from the outside nature and energies of the storm they had survived, Gavin dreamed, the images staying with him, even through the next day's long ride to Old Town Tascosa.

He stood at a precipice.

The wind howled around him as he gazed down into the deep, bottomless pit before him. It looked like the Grand Canyon in Arizona, but more hellish than the real thing. He couldn't see the bottom.

Suddenly, he felt an itch between his shoulder blades. He ignored it at first, thinking it was like the proverbial itch when someone was drawing a bead on you, rifle barrel pointed at your spine.

But the intensity of the feeling soon was too much to ignore, and he caught himself trying to look behind him, to see what was happening to his back.

The itch soon turned to pain. Intense, searing pain, and with it, a feeling of tearing away, and detaching from his own body.

Gavin looked down on himself, rising above his body, and his attention instantly went to his new form.

He was glowing like a campfire. The light seemed to come from within him, and he glanced over his shoulder as he rose swiftly into the air. What he saw made him pause in wonder and awe.

Wide, sweeping wings of large bird feathers, a deep gold and white in color, beat behind him, and as he saw the wings, he could suddenly feel the muscles of his back flexing and retracting, making the outspread wings move in the heavy wind.

He smiled, and as he soon got the natural rhythms and the muscle memory of flying with wings, he soon found himself swooping and spinning all through the air.

And that's when the words formed in his mind, deep within himself.

Not a bird. No. An Angel.

With that, the light within him brightened to an almost blinding glare, and he flew upward at a speed that he had no context to understand.

He soon found the wings behind him paused in their deep sweeps, and his feet alighted on a mosaic floor. Deep golds and whites, matching the colors of his wings, grew outward in concentric circles from where he stood.

He looked down at himself, and everything that made him... well, him, *was gone. His clothing, his pistols, his boots, and canvas clothing. Even the hat he'd had on his head was missing.*

It was all replaced with intense, blinding light. The light made up not only his body, but the clothing that he could still feel against his skin but couldn't see as anything but bright energy.

His attention soon lifted from looking down at himself, and what he saw next shook him so deeply that he awoke back in the warm, comfortable cave, the dream loud in his mind, not allowing him to sleep again for a long while.

Back in the white and gold room, the floor under his bright feet clean and pure, he looked up and beheld a large golden hand. It was outstretched toward him, and the size and awesomeness of it took Gavin's breath away.

And as he watched, fear sprung into his belly, and forced him awake.

The hand uncurled, the long, oversized fingers reaching toward Gavin, and in an almost instant, the giant, metallic golden hand seized the form that was Gavin, squeezing him until he felt ready to pop.

Right before the disturbing dream brought Gavin awake in the cave, he saw his entire life unfold in blinding speed before his eyes, and the golden hand, stronger than a mountain, and wider than a tidal wave, squeezed Gavin, not relenting, and with a scream, Gavin felt crushed unto final and horrible death.

The next day dawned bright and cheery. Everyone was in a great and grand mood, as well as could be expected in Gavin's case because of the disturbing dream, but as they set out to find the road south, bypassing the almost sure death that taking any other path south would provide, his mood cheered quickly.

They found the road within only a few minutes of leaving the cave that had appeared out of nowhere. *That was peculiar*, Gavin thought to himself as they set themselves on the wide, dirt path leading in a winding, almost lazy direction south.

And the dream stayed with Gavin the entire day, repeating over and over in his mind, especially the feeling of being squeezed to death in the vise of the golden hand.

But even more troubling was not so much the conclusion of the dream. That was disturbing enough to recollect all that day, he knew, it was the feeling of the body of energy and light, with the large, out-swept wings, that really stayed with him as the brush-covered landscape moved by slowly under Mabel's hooves all throughout the hot, dry day.

The feeling of having the body of light had seemed so awfully familiar.

And Gavin had no idea, or context, of the reason for that feeling.

The shadows were growing long, and the sun was setting deep into the west with a burst of reds and oranges that made the four men halt their mounts for a few precious moments to enjoy the splendor of God's natural creation.

As they started heading south once again, winding among the small canyons and hillocks leading down to the floor of the Canadian River Valley, the firelight and lanterns of Old Tascosa lit up the darkening evening before them.

All four men were happy to get off of their horses for a few days, and Gavin, at least, was overjoyed that they had made it all this way with only a couple of mishaps. Traveling anywhere in the wilds of the United States was perilous at best.

But they had made it to town and would get two rooms at the inn in town. The inn butted up against the old brick and stone courthouse, but nothing could be done for the attempt of lawful peacekeeping in that courthouse, amidst the lawlessness of post-Civil War confederate states.

Lawlessness was its own kind of trouble, and nothing seemed to be able to cure it, once it set in, like a boil that wouldn't lance. The often disused and abused courthouse, with it's bullet holes, patched up appearance, and disuse was a stark reminder of just where the men found themselves.

With sighs and grunts, the four men unmounted in front of the two-story inn, hitched the horses to the post out front with many other horses stamping in the heat of the evening, and gathered up bedrolls and saddle bags to spend the night in comfort.

Walking into the bustling barroom of the inn, Gavin saw a few familiar faces, but not the one he had hoped to see. And Colt saw a face he had hoped to never see again.

The innkeeper jaunted up to the four men standing sullenly in the entrance way of the room and inquired how he could help.

"Two clean rooms, Barney, and have Cecilia draw some baths in the back room," Gavin told him.

Upon Gavin's speaking to the man he had gotten to know a little a few years back, when he had come through on Army business, recognition dawned on the older man, and with a shock, Barney the innkeeper recognized Gavin Malloy and his brother for who they were.

"Yes, yes sirs, right away, Mr. Malloy, sir," the man mumbled out.

The cat was then out of the bag, and as his name was heard around the noisy, rowdy, dirty, busy, medium-sized room, all of the talking stopped, cards landed on tabletops, glasses were put down, and all eyes turned toward the Malloy brothers.

Gavin and Colt's faces instantly grew hard, waiting for trouble. Last time they had come through town, several locals were killed for their troubles, and thus the Malloy's were well known, and even more hated.

A tense silence permeated the room for several seconds as both sides of the room decided how they were going to handle the uncomfortable situation, and Gavin's hand hovered lightly over the pistol grip on his right hip.

When several men around the room saw his willingness to draw down, and knowing his reputation, many eyes went right back to what they had been doing, and the din in the room slowly picked back up.

That was, except for one pair of eyes, eyes that belonged to the face that Colt had noticed first, the face of the man who slowly walked up to the four men, his own hands hovering on polished walnut grips that were famous the country over.

Colt spoke first, as he had been the one who had taken this particular set of eyes' uncle's life, four years prior.

The boy had turned into a hard man, and even the Malloy brothers had heard the stories of Jesse James from the Missouri Territory.

"Jesse," Colt spoke, moving in front of his brother and their friends. "We don't need no trouble."

"No trouble, Colt Malloy," Jesse James said, hands still lightly brushing the pistol grips hanging from his skinny hips.

"No trouble at all," he said, with a flick of his eyes and a lightning quick jerk of both hands.

But Gavin Malloy was faster and had always been.

As Jesse James skinned his twin Colt pistols, Gavin's arm, holding his own pistol, fell on Colt's shoulder, his saddle bags hitting the floor a second after Gavin's sights were pulled straight on Jesse's forehead.

Jesse James, famous outlaw, just smiled at the three pistols pointed at him. He returned his own guns with the grin widening on his pretty-boy face.

"Was jus' wonderin' if you still had the draw on me, Gavin Malloy," Jesse said through the smile.

"Come on, let's get a drink!" he said, a little too loudly.

As Jesse James turned back to the room, Gavin saw the Kid's posse, five ugly, burly men in the corner, also holstering drawn pistols.

And with that, the room went right back to normal, as if the Angel of Death had not appeared out of the darkening night, and blood almost run rampant in the streets of Old Tascosa.

Blood spilt rampant, like it did every time the Malloy brothers came round, a'knockin'.

Chapter 14

The four cowpokes-turned-rescuers slept in a bit the next day after their month's long ride south to find the first clue to where to begin looking for young Rye Harrison.

They had all enjoyed washing off the dust and dirt of the ride south the night previously, and had slept fitfully, in spite of the outlaws and bandits now being fully aware of the Malloy brothers being back in town.

The four men were still up early enough, dressed and rested, to enjoy the tail end of Cecilia's famous breakfast spread at the Tascosa Inn.

As the boys set to with heaping plates of homemade biscuits and gravy, crispy bacon, and grits made two ways, Gavin took the opportunity to ask Barney the whereabouts of old Archer Wisdom, the revival preacher that Gavin had spent an ill-fated month with, recovering from a bullet wound to the gut, during the summer of '64.

The bullet had come from a hidden corner right down the street from where Gavin now sat enjoying his bacon.

He had been on the hunt for a rather dangerous conscription dodger named Royce Bergins.

Royce not only dodged his duty to the Army, he then went on to rape and murder the women and children at two homesteads near the Red River. That, Gavin thought when he took on the assignment, wasn't going to be tolerated.

And so, they had sent the Malloy brothers.

Problem was, Royce got the jump on them here in old Tascosa, and Gavin got a gut shot wound as payment for tracking him here. But Archer had patched up old Gavin Malloy that summer, and he did it while singing old gospel songs, and preaching at the Malloy's every chance he got.

Come to find out, Archer Wisdom was still right where Gavin had left him. He made plans over the heavy breakfast with his brother and friends for heading down to the old man's church home.

The sun was warming the surrounding valley floor nicely as the men set out from the wooden-planked front decking of the Tascosa Inn and headed down toward the bottom of the flats, where the river flowed swiftly, swollen from the Rocky Mountain snow melts the winter before.

The cottonwood trees were deeply green, shading the wide trail through the woods down to the quick flowing Canadian River. The deep, burnt red clay of the valley floor, and therefore the color of the water itself, stained everything around the wide banks and sawgrasses, cattails, and weeds.

Amongst all that greenery and swift-flowing red water was a gray, worn-down old church that had seen better days. The high steeple had bird-dropping stains, and the clapboards were falling off into the red water, which rose uncomfortably close to the back side of the old building.

Archer Wisdom had joked that both the church, and he, were going to 'wash away on home' one day.

It looked a lot more like a home to Gavin however, and his step quickened to get inside and see his old mentor.

The cicadas sang loudly, and the sun beat down from almost directly overhead as the sweaty group of men walked up onto the rickety front porch of the old church. Their boot heels raised such a loud ruckus, an angry shout sounded from deep within the dark building, making them all smile.

A general sense of unexpected peace had always surrounded the old church and yards, which was still wholly evident, and Gavin's spirits lifted immediately.

The thin screen door slammed open with a loud bang, and the old man himself, Archer Wisdom, the great prospector-turned-revival preacher, appeared, glaring at the group of them for interrupting his quiet, noontime devotions.

A smile broke the cragged, heavily-lined face, however, as soon as his sharp, bright blue eyes fell on Gavin Malloy.

"Well, I'll be darned, if it ain't Gavin Malloy, in the flesh," the old man cackled.

Still laughing and dancing a little gig, the short, bent-over man with flowing, long white mustaches and an even longer beard met Gavin halfway on the popping and sighing front porch, and they hugged like the old friends that they were.

Pulling back with a heavy sigh, Gavin looked down at his old friend and patted him loudly on the shoulder. Archer beamed up at the taller man for a few more seconds, and then turned, ushering them all inside the cool, dark open room of the church hall.

The pews were lined up in twos up both sides of the shadowy room, and the men followed Archer to the front of them.

They sat down, all in a row, Archer letting out a loud sigh. He pushed a battered and dog-eared Bible out of the way, and finally looked with contentment at the four young men.

"So, how'd I get so lucky to be seeing one of my best friends?" Archer Wisdom asked Gavin.

Gavin smiled back at the older man, feeling the same sense of peace he always did when stopping in to see the preacher. And not just when he was recovering from a gut shot.

As Gavin remembered the reason for their visit, however, his smile faltered, and he glanced down at his dusty boots. The dust was red, which he remembered all too well from his last visit. The red of the panhandle clay got on everything.

He looked back up at his old friend and sighed mightily.

"We need to find Stace Lynn, Archer," he said.

He watched as Archer Wisdom searched his own eyes, trying to figure out what the old man's goddaughter had done now.

Archer Wisdom's eyes grew narrow, and he looked from Gavin to Colt sitting next to him, and the other two men with them, all carrying at least a pistol or two.

"You gonna kill her?" Archer asked him.

"Honestly, Archer, don't know. She kidnapped a girl. Her daddy is big brass with the Army. He wants his baby back, and the lady who done it dead," Gavin told the man.

He never could lie to the preacher.

Archer surprised them all. As he looked over at the four men, trying to decide whether to give up a woman who had gone a bad way, still, he loved her. And he didn't want to see her dead.

"Pray with me," he told the group.

They were all a bit shocked but bowed their heads respectfully as Archer started intoning a prayer to the Almighty.

"Ye ole' Creator, King of the Universe, hear your poor son's prayers, and grant us what we ask," he started.

"We know we go astray, and we ask that you shepherd us back to your will, King of the Heart," he continued praying.

The men were getting uncomfortable. They had never been big on praying for things. But Archer made it quick.

"Forgive us for our sins, our killin', and our fears. And let us know the right way ta' go," he finished. They all repeated the 'amen' after the old man ended the short prayer.

Archer sighed loudly, and patted Gavin on the knee, sitting next to him.

"I heard what she did, Gavin Malloy," Archer finally said. He sighed again. It sounded to Colt and the boys like it pained the old man to give Gavin the information they all needed.

"I know Stace Lynn Craves done gone bad. I know," he said.

Gavin silently let the man continue in his own speed.

"The girl is still alive, and when you find them, I want you to make sure ever'one stays the same." He looked at Gavin sharply. "Don't kill her, Gavin," he finished.

Gavin looked deep into the old man's eyes. He warred between what the general had told him to do to anyone who had kidnapped his little girl and his own want and desire to listen to Archer and make the old man happy.

Finally, his conscience won out.

"Alright Archer, tell me where Snakebite went with the girl, and I'll make sure she lives through it," he told the man. Archer smiled.

"But," he warned the old man, "she draws down on us, and the girl's at risk, I can't promise anything."

Archer Wisdom, the smartest and most respected man that Gavin had ever met, simply nodded, patted Gavin on the knee again, and told the group of men where they would find Snakebite McGee and Rye Harrison.

As they were leaving the old church, Gavin looked back one last time at his old friend.

He wished that he could stay and continue talking to the old man. He promised himself that if he lived through returning the girl to her father, he would come back here for a long visit.

And as the men saddled up, he finally realized that he had never heard from Archer Wisdom just *why* Snakebite had kidnapped the girl.

Guess he would find out when he found the two women, he thought to himself as they trotted out of town, with not a person or thing stirring at their abrupt departure and lack of killing anyone this time around.

The question of motive on Snakebite's part bugged him all the way to New Mexico and beyond.

As he watched the four men walk back up the wide path leading toward town, Archer Wisdom sighed deep in his mortal soul and glanced out at the quickly flowing red waters of the Canadian River a few feet away. The eddies and currents twisted this way and that, hiding quicksand bars and channel catfish.

His deep sapphire eyes pierced through the Material and into the Spiritual, seeing His ArchAngel Host questioning exactly what He was doing, and He knew that He would need to spend more time here in the Material, assuring the success of the rescue of Rye Harrison.

Plans within plans, the Creator of the Universe thought to Himself as He walked back into the old, rickety church, humming a gospel song that was a century or more from being written as He settled back into the front pew.

He picked up the old, battered Bible, and turning to a few favorite passages, smiled in His ease, enjoying the short vacation away from the Celestial War raging in the Planes above, below, and around Him, and of which only He could see.

Chapter 15

Stace Lynn Craves didn't want to be a bad person.

But the voices wouldn't shut up or go away. And so she just kept them quiet by doing their bidding.

That's how she had gotten the reputation that went along with her outlaw name.

Snakebite McGee.

The name had angered her so much when she first heard it, back when she had done almost nothing to deserve it.

So, she had made up the difference in deserving it, in spades, ever since. She had left lots of bodies in her wake, on purpose, and at the whims of those same voices.

She walked to the back of the dark, dank cave. Anger, frustration, and the constant pain that pervaded her every thought made her want to kill something.

To hurt something as badly as she always hurt deep within.

Sunlight filtered in, showing the swirling dust motes in the stale air, caught in the beam of light from a crack in the rocks far overhead. She gingerly stepped around the sunlight hitting the floor of the large rock room.

The unconscious girl was laying on a stone shelf near the back of the cave, behind some needed supplies Snakebite had stolen on her trip out west.

She wanted to kill the beautiful young woman, but the voices had told her in painful shouts not to harm a hair on her pretty auburn head.

Snakebite looked down at her own moleskin clothing, holes showing through where she hadn't mind to patch or sew.

She felt dirty and ugly standing before the prone, sleeping woman, but she was used to that feeling. She even reveled in it.

She knew she had earned every bit of those negative and dirty feelings for herself.

She still itched to kill the woman, though.

The unconscious woman had never woken up from the night that Snakebite had snatched her from her bedroom, with the help of two men she had also left behind her on the trail.

She kicked herself for doing that. The woman's body had been a heavy burden for her ever since.

But she adhered to what the voices told her to do.

Always.

She sniffed loudly down at the young woman, overcame the urge to allow one of her pets to lick the graceful neck of the unconscious woman, and turned on her heels to find her six shooters and clean them.

She had a feeling something, or someone, was coming.

Stace Lynn Craves, aka Snakebite McGee, spread her large oilcloth over a rock situated almost dead center in the deep, dark cave, the sunlight streaming down to her left.

She took out an assortment of pistols and one sawed-off shotgun, and went about stripping, cleaning, and re-assembling her guns.

If life had taught her anything, it was to always keep her weapons well maintained and hidden.

Just like her babies.

She could hear a faint rattle as she finished up cleaning her ivory-handled Colts.

Bertha was awake, and probably hungry. The large rattler was her prized baby, and she always kept the momma fed.

Finishing up her work, Stace Lynn folded the large piece of oily canvas, tucked it away in her belongings, and approached the shelves of heavy white boxes that leaned heavily against one far wall.

The boxes had always cost her dearly, but who could put a price on passion and love for her children?

The topmost box held her biggest snake. Bertha, the diamondback rattlesnake.

She had caught Bertha on a large cliff overlooking the Canadian River, the last time she had visited her father at Old Tascosa. She still remembered the trip with both relish and trepidation.

She reached into an old Army ammo box and pulled out a fat rat by its tail.

The rodent screamed as it smelled its death looming. Snakebite was quite adept at catching fat rats in caves like the one she currently called home. Bertha liked her food alive before she killed and ate it.

She opened the heavy flaps of the top box and dropped the squirming rat right on top of old Bertha. Lightning quick, the rattler caught the rat in her large mouth, fangs dripping venom. The rat had never had a chance.

That made old Snakebite cackle in glee.

Smiling to see her oldest and biggest baby fed, she moved methodically down the row of boxes, feeding her various and assorted babies to assure they lived for and loved her as much as she did for them.

She had always had an affinity for belly-crawling reptiles.

Finishing up with her box of baby coral snakes at the bottom, she straightened back up and saw movement from the corner of her eye.

She was instantly on alert and pulled a pistol from a holster at the small of her back.

She thought maybe the woman had awoken for the first time in a month but then thought otherwise.

The loudest of the voices had assured her that the young woman would stay in what he had called 'suspended animation.'

All Snakebite had had to do was clean up the woman's normal body functions, and turn her every once in a while so she didn't get sores on her body parts against the rock.

She had no idea what the movement was, but other than lugging the heavy, corpse-heavy body around, the woman had not so much as stirred an eyelash.

But then Snakebite saw a dark, evil shadow detach itself from the far back wall, also avoiding the ray of sunshine beaming down on the middle of the compacted dirt floor, and approach her slowly.

All she could hear were the sounds of her babies, her many poisonous snakes as they responded to the large, dark shape moving toward her.

Instantly, she knew who it was, and why her snakes were making every kind of noise of which they were capable.

She was afraid Big Bertha would knock over the entire haphazard stack of oily white boxes.

She hadn't seen the giant demon since she had been a young woman barely old enough to understand what was happening to her. The memories still brought shivers to her spine and wetness to the place where her legs met.

His skin was a deep, dark russet color, and he stood at least eight feet tall.

Naked except for a loincloth that didn't quite hide what slithered underneath, his penetrating glare caused her to nonetheless prostrate herself on the floor, taking her eyes instantly off of his red, lantern-like ones.

His voice sounded in her mind, just as it had for so many years, ever since that encounter when she was barely old enough to bleed her monthly.

"Ahh, little one, still wet and ready for me, as you always were, aren't you?"

His booming, oily voice sounded like the rubbing together of snakeskins and made her shiver in painful ecstasy.

"Yes, Father," was all she could mutter.

The chilly goosebump-causing pleasure racked her body. He knew what he did to her; she knew that deep in her soul. Yet, she could never keep herself away from the thoughts and fantasies of the only time she had seen the demon in the flesh.

She had only been twelve, but it had changed the course of her life forever.

She prepared herself now for her rewards for vigorous obedience and slavery to the giant demon.

She flipped herself over, awaiting his entry into her body. She wore no woman's frippery under her ragged dress, so it would be easy access to one such as the demon.

She had kept herself consecrated for the demon, never letting another man touch her since the overlarge beast had taken her innocence as a young girl.

But as the demon hovered over her prone body, a bright and glorious light from the cave entrance blinded them both.

She spun around on her back in time to see something she couldn't quite make sense of.

Snakebite's mind had been wrapped up in darkness for so long that the light of Glory blinded her more senseless than the sexual, dark ministrations of her demonic father.

A figure stood in the entrance to her cave home. The only place she had felt safe for many years.

At first she couldn't quite place who it was, but then her eyes widened as she heard the giant demon still standing over her gasp in surprise and pain.

She looked up at the large demon who had filled her mind for all of her life with promises and commands.

And that's when she saw a long, silvery metal object sprouting from the demons chest, and barely rolled out of the way as caustic and acidic blood boiled the ground where she had just lay, awaiting the pleasure and pain of her demon lover.

The same demon lover whose body now thudded over, the long, overly bright object still sprouting from his large, expansive chest.

"Ahh, well now, that metal worked perfectly. I'll have to tell my Children," a familiar voice said from the entrance.

She had almost forgotten the man bathed in bright glorious light.

She turned, finally recognizing the voice. It was her godfather. The man who had been more father to her throughout her life than any biological man.

"My child," he said to her silence and shock.

"My child," Archer Wisdom repeated from the doorway of the cave, "why dost thou lay with hell spawn?"

She couldn't take her eyes off of him except to look back at the large beast whose voice was now deadly silent within her mind.

"Daddy?" she asked, still shocked at what she beheld before her.

Her godfather, the revival preacher known as Archer Wisdom, still looked down at her where she crouched.

The kindness in his eyes was too much for her to take.

She felt suddenly flayed open for all the world to see. Her mistakes, her sins. Her very soul, darkened and poisoned by a lifetime of slavery to the demonic thrall.

She wept tears of hot acid at the sight of her godfather.

And then revelation overcame her, and she knew that she did not look at her father in the figure in the doorway.

She was looking at the very opposite of the voices that had plagued her since she was a young girl.

She was looking at God Himself, and she fell to her face, too dirty to occupy the same place as the Holiest of anyone of which she had ever heard.

Years of conversations and warnings from the man who stood before her, yet didn't, crowded out the dark and evil sounds within her soul and mind.

And with that knowledge, and now a new, gentler and easier voice pervading her mind, she found herself wrapped up in His arms, being comforted like a child.

A child she found herself becoming once again, as she had been before the demon had stolen her innocence.

Her Father comforted her, soothed her, and after what seemed like eternity, left her to look after her new ward, her new commands easy and light.

The woman. And the men who would be coming looking for her. She was to protect the woman until the men found them.

God had told her the entire plan, deep in her newly whole and healed and soul.

Soon, she found herself humming some old song her earthly father had taught her as a child as she moved around the large cave, getting it ready to receive the guests who would be arriving soon.

She knew only three of the four men would arrive at her cave in a few weeks' time. She needed to make sure they were all comfortable when they arrived.

They would be sorely down and needing a satisfying meal and an even better piece of news after losing one of their own. She looked forward to telling them the Good News.

Her Father had told her that the men didn't know what would happen quite yet, but she was to tell them what to expect afterward.

She hummed the old battle hymn as her Heavenly Father beamed down on her, taking the deceased demon with Him back to the Heavenly Realms to study, in hopes of finding a new source of Heavenly weaponry based on what He and His Children could learn.

They had yet to capture a Watcher, and He did not want to miss the chance to turn the tides of the Battles to Come.

The Creator caught Himself humming the same battle hymn as He ascended to the Spiritual Plane, His plans coming to fruition nicely, indeed.

Chapter 16

The one solid rule of life, according to Gavin Malloy, who had spent most of his adult life on one trail or another, hunting prey who didn't want to be found, was that you couldn't plan for everything.

Especially when a cascading series of events seemed determined to derail everything the group of cowboys was trying to accomplish.

They had set out early the morning after seeing old Archer Wisdom and headed straight south, toward the bustling cattle and oil town of Amarillo. Gavin wanted to see some old friends and resupply. This would be their first chance to use the Bills of Lading that the US Army had given them in their quest to locate and rescue the general's daughter.

Arriving in Amarillo, they settled in an old inn on Polk Street and watched the heavy bustle of the town from the balcony overlooking the brick-laid street.

They felt like real city slickers for the first time in their lives.

Heath, more than the others, was ready to explore the sprawling town, and was raring to get to having a little fun after more than a month on the trail.

But Gavin and Colt both gave him warnings about what to expect, and what not to do, even if he had gotten hard into the whiskey. They had both been to Amarillo before, and knew that if you weren't careful, you'd end up buried in the wrong side of Boot Hill Cemetery.

Heath didn't have a mind to listen, however.

And so, Gavin and Colt found themselves that night at the sheriff's station, giving word of bond so they would release a beat-bloody Heath Kirkeby.

But the night would prove cruel, and fate wouldn't allow just a little blood to run this time.

They left the sheriff's station together, feeling surprisingly good about getting Heath out on verbal bond, only to run into the same band of outlaws who had served Heath his beating to begin with.

The night was dark, but the gas-lit lanterns at every street corner in the town lit up the windy night almost as bright as day. It was warm, and spirits in the loud, growing town were high.

Which, in Gavin's estimation, always made for rough times around the lower-end kinds of folks, like roughnecks and roustabouts.

After the War, money was loose and easy in the sprawling panhandle town, and where there was loose money, warm, windy nights, and whiskey flowing like rivers, people were bound to get hurt at the very least, dead at the most.

The pain was evident on Heath's face, his body held up between the two brothers, as they meandered down the middle of a dirt side road off the main throughfare of Polk Street.

They walked through the islands of light thrown off by the many gas lanterns sitting atop metal poles, but the darkness in between the circles of light was deep as black ink.

It was from one of those in-between points of darkness that four men walked out between two wooden buildings, as if they had been waiting for the trio.

Gavin Malloy swore under his breath, suddenly wishing they had not left Russ back at the hotel watching their belongings and horses.

Gavin and Colt were both immediately aware of the danger and didn't hesitate when the men all went for their pistols. They dropped their best friend to the dirt under their dusty boots and skinned their pistols all in smooth, practiced movements.

Before the smoke from the discharged rounds had dissipated, four roughnecks lay bleeding and dying the in the west Texas dirt, and the brothers were moving once more with their wounded best friend, back to the inn on Polk Street, and to get the hell out of Dodge before the dead bodies were laid at their feet, a lynch mob right behind them.

Even in a large, bustling town, people saw things, and word always came back against strangers.

Gavin knew his visiting with old friends and gathering supplies would have to wait a few more days.

The four men, three holding up the wounded fourth, were away from Amarillo, toward the darkness to the west, and away from the town where four murders would have had them strung up that very day, within an hour.

They moved west at as fast a clip as they dared, the shadows growing before them from the rising sun at their backs.

Arriving in the small, single-road township of Vega, Texas, they were finally able to rest their legs and their backsides, lay up for a night or two, and resupply at the Army Depot nearby.

Finally, Gavin's mind could rest and stop stressing and worrying over leaving bodies behind them in their wake, while they pursued a single gal who didn't mean anything to any of them.

They had been going fast and strong for more weeks than he cared to remember, and he knew he needed a time to get away, sit looking at something pretty, and let his mind settle the doubts, worries, and fears that made him react in such rash ways like they had back in Amarillo.

And he really need to chew on all that Archer Wisdom had told him about Snakebite, and the girl they were supposed to rescue.

It hadn't sat right with him the whole time, and he needed some downtime to figure things out before moving into New Mexico Territory, and toward a dance with fate.

Chapter 17

Just to the north of the small, one-horse town of Vega, Texas, was a smaller version of the vast Palo Duro Canyon that was situated to the south, and which Gavin had only visited once before, on a search for an Indian warrior called Jumping Bear.

The arroyos here were deep, and the mesas were wide in this part of the world. The land was desert-like, and the scrub brush and barely-waist-high stunted trees reminded Gavin of the lesser parts of the world. There was not a lot of green around him.

This landscape was mostly tans of various shades, and deep, dark red soil.

It was such a vast difference to the tall, open skies, deep woods, and soaring mountain ranges of Montana Territory, that sometimes being this far south, Gavin Malloy found himself sick in his midsection to be back home.

But they had a job to do here-abouts, and he meant to see it done.

To the top of one such mesa, Gavin resolutely rode, to get his head wrapped around all that had happened, and what they would be marching into in the next week or so.

The sky overhead was cloudy, and a deep shadow seemed to lay over the land around him. The wind was strong, biting his face and hands with small bits of gravel and grit.

He squinted his deep blue eyes against the shower of rubble raised by the powerful wind, and determinedly faced to the north, and back toward home.

He, of course, could not see all the way to the Montana Territory, but he knew which direction it was in, and God willing, he and his brother and friends would get back there in one piece, sooner than later.

He closed his eyes tightly against the blaring sun overhead, felt his mare settle under him, and listened to the wind as his mind scattered and thought back over the last several days' worth of information. Information that he had not allowed himself to assimilate up until this moment.

He saw the previous gun fights from the last week in his mind's eye suddenly and flinched as the roar of the pistols and rifles sounded loudly in his memory.

Bodies falling every which way was no new experience for the experienced killer, but it had been some time since he had killed a man, and Gavin had hoped against hope that he had put that time of his life behind him.

He felt his soul settle within himself in the hot sun and warm wind around him.

This was the part of the trail that he enjoyed the most. When he knew that any new evil he purported on this earth could in no way equal or add to what he had done in his previous life, and therefore, he became okay with what he'd had to do recently.

His mind went quickly to thoughts of his childhood, disrupted by the Civil War and the loss of their parents. His mother and father had both been consumed and died from a pneumonia that had gone around the territory, both in the same winter. He didn't think of them much, but he knew that Colt thought of his parents most days. Gavin tried his best to just focus on the here and now, but the past always reared it's ugly head, and it was usually at the thought of all the bodies he had left laying in dirt and mud behind him.

His bloody butcher's bill was high, but going to hell was nothing new to the lean, rugged man.

He knew it didn't matter how many more souls he added to that list. He was destined for damnation no matter what he did now.

Mabel moved slightly under him, reaching down to munch some of the dense scrub grasses under her hooves.

He let her graze as he kept his eyes closed tightly against the bright sun and the dark memories.

He put the thoughts of death behind him with resolute grit, forcing his mind to turn forward, and to try to plan out what was ahead of them as they rode into New Mexico and the fate that awaited them as they searched for Snakebite and the general's daughter.

And as soon as his mind settled on a preliminary course of action, two things outside of his closed eyes happened simultaneously, and shattered the thoughts he had been mulling over.

First, Mabel reared up on her hind legs like she had been bit by a rattler and dumped him square on his hind end on the soft dirt of the mesa, and at the same time, a bright light, outshining even the sun, shone down on the spot where his normally calm, peaceful horse had just stood.

Both events shattered the tranquility Gavin had only just obtained in his mind, and as he got to his feet, he skinned both pistols from the leather holsters at his hips.

The bright light in front of him turned into a human-shaped Being of grotesque size and proportions, floating in mid-air, with long, dark-blue wings extended to both sides.

Gavin couldn't set a sex to the Being, as it displayed both male and female parts on its dark blue, muscular form.

And with each beat of the Being's gigantic, bird-like wings, gusts of warm, dust-filled wind pushed into Gavin's face.

Gavin, pistols in hand, and the giant Being hovering several feet in the air in front of him, just stared at each other, time seeming to stand still.

Gavin felt the previous, slightly tenuous grip on his mind shatter into a thousand jagged pieces as the dark Being suddenly smiled down at him, large teeth like square, even tiles of ivory flashing in the afternoon sun.

The Being lifted both hands, in a display probably meant to keep Gavin from panicking and running after his horse, but when Gavin saw the Being's fingertips ending in long, metallically-sharp blades, he did just that.

Terror overcame Gavin Malloy, the fastest gunman in the West, and he suddenly knew that the butcher's bill that he had just been ruminating over was finally coming due.

Death was finally here to harvest his soul, and usher him down to where there was torturous wailing, and the gnashing of teeth.

Chapter 18

"Hold, gunslinger, hold!"

A loud, masculine voice ricocheted around Gavin's mind as he scrambled in the loose dirt and gravel to find purchase and get away from the flying monstrosity.

Just the sound and volume of the voice in his mind made Gavin pause in his tracks. He looked back over his shoulder at the tall Being still floating in mid-air, great wings beating in time with Gavin's own heavy breathing.

A cloud blew in front of the sun suddenly, and it only made the bright light seemingly coming from behind the Being brighter, and Gavin had to shade his eyes with his hand.

That's when he realized that he had dropped both of his pistols in his panic to get away from the nightmare before him.

He moved his eyes down to the ground, searching desperately for his weapons.

The voice sounded loud in his mind again, making him flinch behind the hand shading his eyes from the brightness of the Being.

He kept his shaded eyes on the ground, though, not able to find his pistols and filled with a new panic for it.

"Hold, little brother. We must speak of things to come," the voice echoed in his head.

How it was able to talk to Gavin's mind, he couldn't fathom, and the unfamiliar thoughts were so alien, he was suddenly dizzy.

He looked back up at the floating nightmare and could physically feel his heartbeat slow down as the Being slowly fell downward, coming to light on the loose dirt atop the tall mesa.

Once Death itself folded its large, outstretched wings inward, the Being only became a seven- or eight-foot-tall being, loosely dressed, and looking down on Gavin with an almost whimsical expression on its gender-neutral face.

"I am not now, nor have I ever been mistaken for Death," the Being spoke in Gavin's mind again.

Gavin still felt light-headed and only wanted to find his pistols and get them back in his holsters. He felt naked without their familiar weight on his hips. Again, he found his thoughts spinning and couldn't settle on his current situation.

"She had other things to do this morning," the Being laughed.

Gavin felt his bowels loosen and a hard, raspy swallow made his throat hurt in its dryness.

Taking a deep, cleansing breath, Gavin got his nerves and shock under control with an iron will, and watched as the large Being watched him. They locked eyes across the short distance between them, and Gavin's heartrate started leveling out. And a knowing smile again crossed the tall Being's face.

"You're an angel, aren't you?" Gavin finally asked.

The tall Being looked back over its shoulder, seeing its wings folded neatly at its back, and then down at itself, as if seeing itself from Gavin's perspective.

Finally it spoke.

"I'm a little more than that, gunslinger," it said out loud.

Gavin was shocked that the Being's voice was more feminine out loud than it had been in his mind.

"You would call me an ArchAngel, although we have other names for ourselves," the Being said.

"My name is Raguel, and I am God's Justice." Finality sounded loudly in the Being's tone.

Gavin didn't like that last part. Not one bit.

"Then you are here to kill me?" Gavin asked, suddenly nervous all over again.

He shuffled his feet, raking his boots through the dust and dirt, hoping to feel his pistols under him, without taking his eyes off of the tall Being before him.

"While that would be my normal Mission, no, gunslinger," the ArchAngel answered him.

"I am actually here to assure you live until your own mission is complete."

"Mission?" Gavin asked. "What mission?"

The ArchAngel looked down at him for a long, uncomfortable moment.

Finally coming to some conclusion in its mind, it smiled at Gavin again, and gestured to the same dirt- and dust-covered ground at the top of the mesa upon which they both stood, and that Gavin was shuffling through, searching for his damn guns.

"Let's sit, shall we?" the ArchAngel said. "I will tell you of the fight we all have before us."

Gavin simply nodded and directed his attention to the ground around him, hoping to finally find his matching pistols. He was cursing under his breath as his eyes scanned the ground.

He finally spied both pistols stuck within a tall yucca plant several feet from where he was standing.

He was momentarily preoccupied with wondering how they had flown so far from his hands when he had dropped them. Gavin didn't think he had spooked that bad.

He walked the few steps to the tall, spindly plant, retrieved his pistols, and then pushed them both into the holsters on his hips with a sigh of relief.

Not that the guns would matter much against an agent of the Almighty, he thought, but he was still glad to have the weight of them on his hips once again.

And that's when he remembered that Mabel, his normally placid horse, had run off, spooked by the Heavenly entity waiting patiently behind him.

He looked down at the base of the tall mesa, and saw Mabel, munching some prairie grasses like nothing miraculous or life shaking had just happened up at the top where Gavin stood.

He decided that she was fine where she was, with her reins trailing down on the ground around her, and her saddle sitting empty on her back.

Gavin turned back to the tall ArchAngel, and shock and awe blossomed in his chest once again.

The tall, gender-neutral Being who had set down on the mesa just a few moments before, was now displayed as an entirely different person altogether.

The Being must have transformed as Gavin's attention was focused on finding his pistols.

Because before him now was a man of middle height, middle looks, and middle weight, wearing unfamiliar clothing, and sitting at a metal table of some kind.

He was drinking something dark out of a white porcelain tea cup and looking rather too comfortable in the West Texas heat of the day.

"Sit down, gunslinger, and let's talk," this new man told Gavin, nodding at the chair that materialized on the other side of the round, white, metal table before him.

And so, Gavin sat, if only to hear what this fantastic Being had to say to him.

Gavin hoped with the lightheadedness he felt and the surrealness of the situation, he would walk out of this alive and fully intact. As he took his seat, he knew that he was thinking of his mind, and not so much his body.

The ArchAngel smiled over at Gavin, and a tall cup, the likes of which he had never seen before, appeared on the table in front of him, a dark amber drink filling it. It was painted garishly bright, but in a way that seemed very foreign, and almost European to him.

The ArchAngel smiled at him. "It's a German stein of beer; drink it, you'll enjoy it."

Gavin looked at the ArchAngel sitting comfortably in the bright sunlight with doubt, but still saw his own right hand reaching out to the metal stein and pulling it to his lips, drinking deep of a beer unlike any he had ever experienced.

It was the best tasting thing he had ever put into his mouth, and he drank with deep pulls, emptying the cup in a few seconds.

He set it back down, empty, on the table, and belched loudly, making the ArchAngel Raguel smile brightly.

Gavin sat back, sated, and gestured with both hands, allowing the ArchAngel to proceed with whatever information he needed to give Gavin.

"You are Gavin Malloy, a gunfighter and bounty hunter of legendary proportions, and I am the ArchAngel given Mission to assure your success in your current endeavors," the ArchAngel said by way of introductions.

"And I'm to watch over you and guide you to make sure that you do not die in the struggle," he said with some finality.

"If you were to perish, a cataclysmic event would wipe out everything that you have ever known, or not known, by an enemy that we still don't know much about," Raguel said finally, looking off into the distance of the late afternoon sky.

"So, to answer your question about this Mission, there you have it," the ArchAngel said, and sat back with some little resignation on his very human, very perfectly symmetrical face.

Gavin looked down at the German stein with a little longing, wishing more beer would magically appear again, and as if his wishes had been heard, the metal cup filled again with the cold, delicious beer.

He didn't reach for the cup, however. He looked back over at the man sitting across the unfamiliar table from him and asked what any sane man would ask in this situation, if he found himself just so.

"What the hell are you talking about, angel?" Gavin asked.

Raguel smiled again at Gavin and Gavin knew the action came easy to the heavenly Being.

"You're to the point as always, gunslinger," Raguel said. "I've always liked that about you."

The ArchAngel sat back in his seat and gestured to the sky overhead.

And like a story from the Bible itself, everything around them froze, including the very clouds in the sky, and the movement of the sun and the wind around them.

"Shall I start from the Beginning then?" the ArchAngel asked.

Gavin simply nodded dumbly, reaching for the newly filled stein of beer, and the hopeful buzz from the alcohol that would shrink the fear he felt growing once again in his belly.

Chapter 19

"The Being that you call 'God,' we refer to as our Father," Raguel explained.

They were still sitting across from each other atop the large, rocky mesa, and Gavin was sipping the cold amber liquid more slowly this time.

"At the beginning of Creation, when our Father formed the universe, and all within, He created several worlds like the one in which we sit," Raguel said.

"Those worlds number eight, and they all exist within what we call the Material Plane of existence, or just 'the Material,'" he said.

Gavin nodded along like he had any idea whatsoever of what the ArchAngel spoke, but he wanted to know everything anyway.

Even if he only understood what the Being said in small ways. The cadence of the ArchAngel's words was mesmerizing.

"As a Host of ArchAngels, me and my brothers and sisters are given Missions to assure that the Father's Will is enacted upon the Material, especially when the Father doesn't want to act Himself," the ArchAngel explained.

"In one such Mission, on a very different world from the one you know, yet so very similar, the Host, and the Father Himself, started noticing something we had never seen before," he said.

"An enemy of unknown origin, yet an enemy all the same, starting attacking and disrupting the Missions," he said.

He had a look of concern on his face the likes of which Gavin had never seen before.

"They even tried to kill our Creator," Raguel said.

He was once again looking off into the distance, seeing memories or situations that caused him physical pain.

"And so, we fought back. We have been doing so longer than I care to remember," Raguel sighed.

Gavin did not want to interrupt the angel's recounting of the past, on these other worlds of which he spoke, but he was itching to learn how all of this information had a single iota to do with him.

He was about to ask the tall Being, but Raguel spoke again, telling Gavin exactly what he wanted to know.

"That brings me to you, and your current situation," he said.

Gavin's ears perked up.

"The Father has chosen you and your brother to complete a Mission of great importance," the Archangel told the cowboy.

"You and Colt are to rescue young Rye Harrison, but in doing so, cause the ire of our enemy, and thus join us in the fight, here in the Material, and help vanquish the enemy here on this planet," he said.

Gavin just sighed loudly.

More fighting was the thought that reverberated in his head, over and over.

"And as you rescue young Rye, you will be gaining the one thing you so desire, Gavin Malloy," Raguel told him.

"You will receive Redemption for all of your past sins," the ArchAngel finally said.

Gavin finally had too many questions rattling around in his mind. He had to ask the one that mattered most to him and his family at that moment.

"Why me, and my brother?" Gavin finally burst out.

The ArchAngel stared at Gavin for several uncomfortable moments, and tilted his head to the side, his left ear lifting to the sky, as if he were listening to instructions or answers from upon high.

Finally satisfied with whatever he heard, he answered Gavin in only the way an Angel could.

"Because, young gunslinger," the ArchAngel answered, "you are to become one of us, when your time on this Plane is done."

"You are to become an ArchAngel, like me, and my brothers and sisters all."

With the sound of a slamming door, Gavin's perception expanded suddenly, and he felt the coils of responsibility and fate intertwined around his soul, drawing him inexorably toward the edge of a destiny in which he didn't choose for himself.

His ranch, and his freedom, had never felt further away from him than they did at that moment.

But finality had never bothered the fastest gun draw in the west, and death was a welcome friend. He just nodded at the ArchAngel, in both resignation and a final, permanent acceptance of who he was and what he was supposed to do.

He looked resolutely at the tall ArchAngel.

Without removing his eyes from the tall Being's bright blue ones, he drained the final few swallows of his still cool beer, and asked the question he knew the ArchAngel wanted to hear the most.

"What do you want us to do, and how do you want us to do it?"

Chapter 20

Back on the trail, the dust and heat rising behind them, along with the memory of meeting the strange Heavenly Being, Gavin felt peace settle into his middle, and looked forward to having this Mission complete.

But knowing what came after, well, that gave the peace inside a bit of a shake, if he admitted it honestly to himself.

He had never minded a fight. But he still had no idea what or where they would be fighting, and the fear in his middle warred with the peace.

As the horses plodded to the west, he looked at his brother, wondering if he should burden Colt with the information he had only just received. As his brother's face grimaced in pain, a pain that was caused from both the night before, and the life behind them, Gavin decided against it.

What Colt didn't know right now wouldn't add to the mental demons he danced with most days. Gavin hated doing that to his brother, and normally wouldn't, but this situation was a horse of a different color.

Heath and his red-headed friend, Russ, were joking and talking between themselves, the bruises on Heath's face starting to fade in the early morning light, and Gavin was glad to have the men along. Thinking of what the ArchAngel had told him about the fighting to come, he would be glad to have men he trusted at his sides and back.

And thinking of the fighting, he glanced around nervously at the flat landscape around them, waiting for demons and black things and even worse, according to the ArchAngel, to jump out at them at any time.

He hoped the paranoia wouldn't stay with him the whole way to New Mexico.

His hope, soon after that thought, turned right to black dread as bullets whizzed between the riders, the loud bangs and lightning flashes fired from unseen pistols and rifles raining down death and hellfire, all around them.

Sheriff Brooks McGurrin was no fool, he whispered to himself.

But he was also extremely lazy, so it would take something like the death of his wife's kid brother to stir him up enough to take to the saddle and ride down some murderin' thugs.

Even if he knew the truth to be that his wife's kid brother was a true derelict and probably started the fight that had got him killed.

His wife didn't none care, and so Brooks found himself horseback riding as fast as he could with five of his hastily deputized friends toward men he sure did not want to mess with.

Brooks McGurrin had stayed alive as long as he had as the sheriff of Potter and Randall counties in the Texas panhandle by not being a fool.

And he sure as hell felt a fool for chasing down men like Gavin and Colt Malloy.

Hell, he thought as he galloped through the morning sunlight and early heat of the day, *he felt downright idiotic trying to think of some way to get the drop on the Malloy brothers.*

He knew he and his deputies, even in an ambush, probably weren't good enough to take down the Malloy boys.

Their only hope, he had told his men, was to get around them, and have them ride into an ambush, and try to kill every single man of the small group before they even knew what hit them.

If the fighting went beyond the first volley of bullets, he had said, they would all be dead, and not the Malloy's, no sir.

The new deputies gathered around the saloon bar the night before would be the ones pushing daisies come the next day.

And now that next day was here, and Brooks sure still felt a damn fool. Better that then a wife with a hornet's nest in her bonnet, however.

The loud staccato of the posse's horse hooves against the heavily dark and hard-as-bedrock dirt to the west of Amarillo sounded like fireworks in his mind, but all he could think about were the things he had heard of Gavin Malloy from during the war.

Hell, he thought, *what they all had heard.*

The man had been a legend for the body count he had amassed as a manhunter for the Union.

And now, here was poor old Brooks McGurrin riding toward hell and brimstone just because his young pretty wife mourned her little brother, the idiot.

She would soon be mourning more than just her little brother, Brooks thought grimly.

He sure didn't feel right about the day.

The posse pulled up atop a hill overlooking the small town of Vega, and watched as the four men who were responsible for his brother-in-law's murder the night before walked their mounts into the heart of the town like they owned the place.

From the stories rebounding in Brooks' head about Gavin Malloy, that picture wasn't too far off the mark.

The posse dismounted back down the hill so as not to present a silhouette against the brightening day and put their heads together over which way the outlaws would go after refitting in Vega.

The consensus was further west, heading toward the border with New Mexico, and evading capture for the murders on the streets of Amarillo.

New Mexico was a lot closer then Oklahoma, one of his deputies said in a quiet whisper. They were all whispering for some ungodly reason. There was no way the men down in the town could hear them.

Those were the only state borders around the rectangle of the panhandle, and the outlaws would be pushing hard for it, Brooks and his deputies knew.

"Good, good, let's get ahead of them before they hit the border, and waylay them in the hills," Brooks told the deputies.

As they remounted to continue running west, Brooks was happy to see he wasn't the only man shaking in his boots.

Gavin Malloy, and his big brother Colt, had such an overwhelming reputation for killing from the War, that not a man amongst them wanted to square dance with the pair.

Brooks himself had heard about the Malloy brothers causing such death and strife all over the south that the streets literally ran red in Tascosa, Tucumcari, Dodge City up in Kansas, and down south in El Paso, near the Rio Grande.

The brothers had been such a two-man band of death and destruction, hunting down deserters and bandits, outlaws, and murders, that not a soldier in either the Confederacy or the Union didn't have fear of the Malloy name.

Brooks didn't know what had happened to the pair since the War and had only ever met them a single time in Amarillo during it, but it was enough to recognize the murderin' eyes of the two men.

He really didn't want to meet those eyes again, for damn sure. But he had, the night his brother-in-law had been killed, as the brothers had picked up on of their own from Brooks' jail.

He didn't remember even uttering a word the night before, as Gavin Malloy stood not three feet from him, Malloy's attention all on his friend, Heath.

Setting up the ambush between two tall, scrub-covered hills, a few miles from the New Mexico border, Brooks could only seem to focus on the bright eyes of the Malloy brothers.

Like a fiery pair of demon eyes in a dark room, he saw their bright blue eyes burning brightly in his memories.

The memory was so jarring that when the time came for the shooting to start, he hesitated just long enough, and so did some of his men, that the first volley didn't do anything more than kill one of the outlaws and piss off all the others.

It was really over before it had begun, but the soon-to-be-expired Sheriff Brooks McGurrin hadn't quite known what that would look like.

All he saw, as he lay in the dirt bleeding from a sucking chest shot, were the bright, fiery eyes of the murderin' Gavin Malloy.

Those icy blue eyes looked down on him, pistol fire making no sound over the buzzing in the sheriff's ears, and as darkness closed in, those blank blue eyes were the last thing he saw this side of paradise.

Those icy, cold, blue eyes followed the late Sheriff Brooks McGurrin all the way to the pearly gates, and for a long while beyond.

Chapter 21

"Get down boys!" Gavin heard himself shouting.

All he heard were bullets, and all he saw was his closest friend, Heath Kirkeby, fall off of his horse clutching himself.

Gavin knew the man was dead before Heath's body hit the hard, dusty ground.

Landing squarely on his boots behind Mabel, Gavin immediately skinned both of his pistols, found immediate cover behind a large boulder that luckily hid him and his horse both, and started shooting back.

Thankfully, he saw that he wasn't the only one who had found cover, was firing back, and was pissed off as hell.

Colt was only a few feet away behind his own sheltering rockfall, and the look of rage and tightness on his face made Gavin once again thankful for having his brother always by his side.

Gavin hit two men squarely before he had fired his first six shots. One in the chest, one in the head.

He vaguely wondered who the men were but had no time to ponder on it. All he knew was that Heath was dead already, and he had better get his shit together so the rest of the crew didn't end up the same way.

He swallowed the dark, depressing emotions surrounding the death of his best friend and got to work.

Honed by years of warfare, training, and natural talent, and bolstered by the lack of fear that he had always had at the core of him, he charged out from where he was sequestered, and had killed or maimed three more men at a dead run toward the very middle of the obvious ambush that had been set for him.

The men had no time to register what they were seeing before they were gunned down by a man who showed no fear in the face of certain death.

And with that lack of fear, the certain death of Gavin Malloy was bequeathed on those attempting to dole it out instead.

Between him, Colt, and Russ the Irishman, the broken ambush was easily overcome within a matter of seconds.

Colt walked up to his brother, holstering both of his own Colt .45s, and shook his head. He had seen the silver stars on all of the dead men's chests.

"Shit, Gavin. The Law," Colt said, wiping his sweaty hands on his dusty shirt.

Gavin felt sweat breaking out in cold chills all over his own body.

"Doesn't matter, Colt, we're on Army business," he told his brother.

"Army business trumps the Law," he said.

They heard a loud sob behind them, and with downcast expressions on both their faces, turned to see Russ bending down over Heath.

Damn it, Gavin thought.

Sudden guilt bubbled up as he realized that he had forgotten in those few moments that their best friend had been shot during the first volley of hot lead from the idiots trying to ambush them.

The sun was high overhead, heat beating down on the group as the brothers walked over to their fallen friend. Gavin looked at the sky and wasn't surprised to already see birds spiraling overhead.

The War, and subsequent lawlessness in the south, had made carrion birds fat with death and destruction. *Animals that survived on death were living mighty fine*, Gavin whispered in his head as he drew near to the body of his dearest friend.

He knew that he was thinking about more than just vultures and coyotes. There were men who lived off death, and he wondered painfully if he was one such.

They removed their hats, knelt down around Heath's body, and forgot for the moment the other bodies strewn around the West Texas hills.

Being so caught up in their own affairs, and not having too much knowledge of what their childhood friend was doing the last few years, Gavin and Colt both felt an extreme sorrow over the sudden and horrific loss of Heath Kirkeby.

Tears shone in both men's eyes, and Colt could think only of a bottle for that night, and the nightmares sneaking in at the edges, once again.

Gavin could only think about how many men and women he had let down, and how many bodies were tallied on his butcher's bill.

He, too, would need a bottle of something strong and mind numbing to be able to sleep that night.

And the Irishman, Russ O'Shanashay, mourned the loss of his best friend, his confidant, and the man that he secretly loved, and who had loved him back in a way that was not allowed in these here wilds of the west.

Tears streaming down his face with the loss of his heart and love, Russ stood, put his hat back on his head, and started looking for a way to get Heath's body away from the circling vultures.

He worried the rest of the day, with his love's bleeding body secured to the horse Russ now led, about finding just the right place to bury a man who had deserved the entire world.

Miles to the west, wearing a simple ranch-style dress that she had gone into some unnamed small town to purchase, Stace Craves was sweeping the dirt floor of the back room, removing loose gravel over the stone of the cave bottom.

With no warning, and with a sudden sharpness, she felt the physical pain of a bullet passing into and back out of her chest and knew instinctively what had happened.

One of the men of the group soon to arrive at her home had been killed, as her Father had shown her so many days earlier.

The shock of the pain took Stace to her knees, where she worried about scuffing up the hem of her new dress and counterbalanced that thought with the drastic difference in who she was now compared to who she had been not too long earlier.

Deep sorrow coursed through her, and her body began to shake. Large, fat tears sprang from both her bright blue eyes.

She knew the pain that the death of one of the men would give to the others.

And she felt it with them.

More would come soon, but in the meantime, she saw the rest of the events of the next several weeks playing out clearly in her mind, over and over.

It wasn't every day that you could see your own death coming swiftly for you, she thought as she stood back up, pain diffusing throughout her body, and began to sweep the gravel and grit from the rock floor of the cave once more.

Not every day, indeed.

Chapter 22

They buried the lawmen close by where their bodies had fallen.

Wasn't no reason to let the vultures and coyotes have at their bodies, Gavin and Colt had agreed. These men, as wayward as they were, deserved proper respect in death.

And so, they were buried as they were, in shallow graves. The three remaining men didn't have all the time in the world to bury dead lawmen.

By the looks of it, these dead men had plans to do the same to the four outlaw men they had tried to ambush, as two of their horses, found nearby, carried short, Army-issued trail shovels.

"Mighty handy, that," Colt had said to Gavin when they found the horses grazing nearby.

"We may want to take them too," he had said, pointing to the six painted mares. "No reason to letting them wander back home, alerting more people to come after us," he finished.

Gavin simply nodded his agreement. He wasn't in the mood for talking. His mind was reeling from everything that had happened since riding into Texas a few days earlier.

The digging took most of the rest of the daylight, and once finished, and the holes filled back in with dead men and dirt, the three, pulling now seven horses and one dead friend wrapped in a blanket found in one saddle bag or another, headed west into the setting sun.

Getting out of Texas, and across the border into New Mexico Territory was of paramount importance to the three remaining men.

The Brothers Malloy knew that where a few lawmen would be on their trail, more would follow. It was as if no one had anything better to do with their time than hamper and impede this journey and quest the men were currently forced to be on.

And the brothers, being on Army business, with letters of transcription, supply, and right-of way stashed in their saddlebags, had thought they would not be impeded. But lawmen bent on justice were sure not known for stopping and listening to reason, letters notwithstanding.

Before nightfall, all three men found themselves over the invisible border, a trail post their only proof they had finally moved out of the Texas panhandle.

Breathing sighs of relief, the brothers set to making camp in the lee side of a large grouping of stones and boulders, the basic spot they had sought out their whole lives, so as to not be seen.

As they moved about with the practiced movements of habit, young Russ pulled down Heath's blanket-wrapped body and moved off into the twilight to find a spot to bury it that only he would know.

The Brothers Malloy didn't mind a bit, now knowing the truth about the pair.

Colt had the small fire started, and a haunch of dried beef, beans, and water slowly boiling in a kettle over it, as Gavin settled the horses, gathered supplies as he could from all the saddlebags and stores of the now deceased lawmen, and went through it all with the practiced and knowledgeable movements of a man who had done the same on several occasions.

The lawmen's supplies and belongings were scant and thin. Meaning, he knew, that they had expected to catch up with the brothers and their friends, ambush them quickly, and be home for supper if they could help it.

Gavin was glad, finally, that they had not been successful. *Overconfident men, out in the wilds, were often dead men,* he ruminated while pulling out dried jerky, tobacco, and a hidden bottle of good whiskey from the sheriff's saddlebags.

After a good, hearty dinner, hot and satisfying, and the return of the Irishman, Russ, the brothers bedded down for the night, having made sure that Russ was doing okay.

The young man was, but barely. Tears shone in the Irishman's blue eyes throughout dinner, and remained there afterward, as the men set about rolling out bedding and settling down for the night. Colt and Gavin both put out the fire, settled all of the horses on a picket line strung between two trees, and got ready the morning fixings for hot coffee and leftovers.

Colt nodded to Gavin before sleep took the younger brother over, assuring him that he would watch over the Irishman through the night. They had whispered together, making a plan to assure the young man would stay the course, even though he had lost the man who had brought him to this particular assignment.

They would still need as many hands, and guns, as they could get. Gavin had a plan for that, settling down on a course of action before sleep overtook him, and another dream took him from the place he was in and brought him to a place he couldn't fathom in his own imagination.

The skies were alive with clashes of light and the booming sounds of crashing weapons. Screams and shouting accompanied the fighting sounds.

Colored blood red, the skies were lowering toward where Gavin stood, atop a tall outcropping, the rocks beneath his boots rugged, and his footing loose.

That forced Gavin to look down at himself and see that he was wearing something that he couldn't wrap his mind around. Armor unlike anything he had ever seen before, yet was overly familiar, and felt like a second skin.

He flexed his arms and legs within the armor, and felt it move around his muscles, the armor reforming with even the slightest movement.

Slung around his hips were his old gun holsters, the leather and metal looking quite alien against the ever-moving armor wrapping his body.

But they felt ever so familiar, and the weight of his guns brought comfort in a very uncomfortable situation.

A scream rent the air around him, causing him to look up and see a nightmare hurtling toward him, blotting out the blood-red sky in front of his rock outcropping.

He pulled both Colt .45s at his hips and blasted the black specter right out of the sky in front of him. Teeth and claws disappeared in the hail of bullets he sent toward the nightmare reaching out for him.

"Good shot, gunslinger," a deep, steady voice said to his left.

He glanced over at the now familiar ArchAngel standing next to him, clad in the same armor as Gavin was, only the Angel's was colored a deep pale blue. Gavin looked back down at his own armor, wondering at the coloring that he saw there.

The moving armor clad to his body, shifting unendingly and protecting him with perfect precision, and feeling like it was made only for him, was colored a bright, shining gold. And that, too, felt perfectly right to Gavin.

"And now, gunfighter, let us join our brothers and sisters in the fight," Raguel said.

Nodding to the ArchAngel standing next to him, Gavin reloaded his pistols with a shake of his wrists, somehow knowing just what to do, and leapt off of the high rock overlook.

He flew up into the air, his brothers and sisters gathered around and behind him. They were the strongest force in all of Creation, and nothing could stop them when Gavin led the Host.

Firing into the horde of darkness in the sky, blood-black ochre spilling from the bodies of the Watchers and Dark Dogs and various other demons attacking his Host, Gavin yelled his lungs out into the cosmos, death and destruction raining from his bullets.

He felt the sword thrusts, and the movement of the other Heavenly Weapons being borne by his brothers and sisters, and grinned at the enemy before him.

Gavin felt right at home amongst the Host, knowing somehow that he was right where he was supposed to be. Right where he was destined to rule, and lead.

Smiling again into the death of the darkness before him, Gavin's feelings of Rightness and Righteousness pervaded his entire countenance, and for the first time in all of his own existence, he felt on the side of Right. He felt fully confident and right at home in the Battle against the Horde.

Coming awake in the deep purple of early morning, Gavin felt like he had slept for three days.

No sounds other than the mating call of insects around the campsite, and the occasional nickering of horses on the picket line, pervaded the temporary serenity of Gavin's mind.

He felt great and knew that his new sense of energy and rest came from the ArchAngel he had met the day before.

Raguel had given him the dream of his future, and finding acceptance in it, Gavin mentally prepared for the day ahead, and the continued trek toward destiny and the many more battles to come.

Part 4
The End of One Road brings the Beginning of Another

Chapter 23

The Malloy brothers brought their line of horses to a scattering halt atop the rise leading down into the valley holding the small town of Santa Rosa, New Mexico.

Newly named thus, the brothers had come to know the town as 'Agua Negra Chiquita,' or 'Little Black Water.'

Glad for the small settlement's name change, memories flooded both men's minds of peace and general ease in their time in the small town, especially in the company of one of their truest friends from back in the War.

They could both see the Pecos River shining in the bright sunlight glaring overhead and looked forward to bathing once again in the cool mountain waters of the large river.

Smiling, Gavin and Colt both whooped as loud as they could and made their way to the only other place on the planet besides their Montana Ranch where they felt at home.

Within a few short minutes, the train of horses, and the three cowboys leading them, pulled up to the largest and tallest of the buildings making up the small settlement, and both brothers smiled up at the chapel of Don Celso Baca, the only man besides Archer Wisdom that they trusted with their very lives.

It had been a hard, heavy ride to the west once the cowboys were assured they were not followed out of Texas, and both brothers could feel the beginning of the end of the trail to find the general's daughter growing closer.

Before that happened, however, Gavin knew that they would need some back-up, and there wasn't a better place to find it than in the home and chapel of their long-time and closest friend, the Don.

Dismounting with a shout toward the tall stucco building, Gavin smiled at his memories of the Don, and the trouble the three of them had achieved chasing some of the worst of the worst criminals and deserters from the Union, who had thought to find safety and comfort in the Mexican outlaw towns of the New Mexico Territory.

Family, friends, strangers, and familiar faces started moving out of the large chapel and home compound of their friend the Don. And the outflow of smiles and laughter made the Malloy brothers' hearts soar.

The Don himself, walking with a cane and being helped by a beautiful granddaughter on his left arm, walked out of the large wooden doors to see the bustle for himself. Upon seeing the brothers dismounting, and grinning themselves, a smile like the heavens lit up the older man's face.

"Mi hermanos!" the older man said with a shout, his smile beaming from ear to ear.

Likewise, the Malloy's found joy and exaltation rebounding in their chests for the man who called them 'brothers.'

"Ya old goot! Good to see ya!" Colt exclaimed, reaching the Don first, having passed through the sea of family and friends to reach the venerable old man.

Clapping the man heartily on the shoulder, Colt turned and stood next to the Don as Gavin approached the small group. Twin smiles lit up both hardened men's faces.

"Don Celso Basa," Gavin said, reaching for the man who had saved his life, thinking as well of the times that Gavin had returned the favor - memories strongly in both men's minds, taking over. It seemed decades in the past, but wasn't all that long ago, and both men knew it.

Embracing tightly, the two men let the kinship and miles of dusty trails they had shared together during the War overwhelm them both, causing them to rejoice in the reunion, too many years in the making.

"Come in, come in, get out of this damn sun," the Don told the cowboys, who graciously accepted. The brothers knew it would be no use trying to unpack their own horses, see to the animal's needs, or even try to repay the Don in any way.

The Don had family and employees enough to see to their every need. And while Gavin told himself they had a mission to complete and couldn't stay past asking for the resources they would need, it was mighty tempting to take the load off, and stay for an extended vacation in the only other place he felt right at home in all the world.

The inside of the palatial and spacious chapel and home residence of the Mexican Don was cool, fragrant, and an oasis compared to the lands and climes the brothers and their compatriots had trod over the last few months, and both brothers breathed deeply the serenity of the place.

Gavin walked with the Don into the inner court of the stucco compound, while Colt fell back and started to speak in Spanish to the Don's wife about the man's health and wellbeing. Gavin knew Colt would fill him in on what the woman said, both knowing the Donà was as much an ally and friend as the Don himself.

Gesturing to a comfortable seat on the veranda overlooking the town the Don had scratched out of the red clay of the Territory, Gavin and Colt both sat with the older man while the family took the Irishman and their belongings deeper into the spacious and comfortable compound.

They would sleep well that night, if nothing else, Gavin thought to himself as he looked out over the work of the town the Don had founded.

"Looks like you've done well here, Celso. Well indeed," Gavin said to his old friend.

The Don simply smiled and nodded, looking out over his town, and back down the memories of all he had accomplished. But not without the help of the two brothers sitting with him, and in no small way either. The Don owed the Malloy's his life many times over, and the debt was owed the other way as well.

Which made for such comfortable and easy companionship, he thought in his astute and wise mind.

The knowing smile was passed around the veranda, in the shade of comfort and ease, while the outside world baked in the harsh overhead sun. The same knowing smile did not break the silence of the moment, until one granddaughter or another of the Don, along with her brothers and sisters, brought trays of refreshments and small snacks for the men to enjoy while talk would drift easily and comfortably for the rest of the hot afternoon, and into the dinnertime hour.

Once the men sitting on the veranda were joined by the Don's two sons, Placido Baca and Crescenciano Baca, who Colt had nicknamed Shooter and Sheriff when they were smaller, the real talk could start, and the brothers could ask a boon of their former captain and brother-in-arms.

Words flowed easily, drinks went down easier, and the night settled in on a tranquility and respite for the cowboys, who beforehand, had found themselves short-winded and exhausted, having run toward a fate neither knew, but which both felt drawn to deep in their weary bones.

Chapter 24

"How many men have you lost then, Celso?" Gavin asked the Don. "Three or four in raids?"

"Más, mi amigo," the Don answered. "Mucho más."

"Jesus," Colt and Gavin said in unison.

They looked over at each other across the veranda, both holding dark bottles of cerveza, and both knowing they couldn't, and wouldn't, get away with not helping their old friend and brother-in-arms.

"I've never seen anything like this, mi hermonos," the Don went on. "Not Val Verde, not with the Navajos. Not even the outlaws on the Santa Fe," he said.

"This Florentine Gonzales Gang is ruthless and deals in blood, Gavin Malloy," the Don said. "I haven't been able to stop them a single time."

The eyebrows of both Malloy brothers rose almost to their hairlines.

That was sure saying a lot, as both brothers were well acquainted with the bloodletting during the short yet brutal Navajo Indian War, as well as what it had taken to break the backs of outlaws hellbent on death and robbery during the trail-breaking work the Don had accomplished early in life along the burgeoning Santa Fe Cattle Trail.

And with all the work that the Don had done in settling the area around his large land grant, saying he couldn't stop this gang of outlaws was an admittance the brothers had never thought they would hear from the esteemed man they thought so highly of.

"But this is my duty and my responsibility, my brothers, please… don't let it bother you," the Don said in that way both brothers knew meant the exact opposite. They smiled low in their beers as the old man pretended to wave away the issues like so much smoke in a strong breeze.

The Don would never let an opportunity for help, especially from men he could trust with his own life, slip by. The Don was no idiot.

You didn't dig a growing, prosperous township out of No Man's Land, holding and protecting it for future generations, by being stupid.

Nor by being afraid to bleed, and to let blood from your enemies.

"Don't you worry none, Celso," Gavin said. Colt nodded along.

"We'll help you out, Lord willing and the creek don't rise."

Don Baca nodded his thanks, knowing he could sure use the help, and also knowing the brothers offered the help out of respect, a sense of responsibility from the past, as well as from deep within souls that the Don, more than anyone else, knew were more good than bad.

"Don't worry, mi hermonos," Don Celso Baca said.

"You help me with this one thing, and I'll make sure to help you find the general's daughter and anything else you may need," he finished.

The Don winked at both men, and burped loudly from the second bottle of beer he had consumed.

Setting down the empty bottle on the table next to him and wiping the sweat from his brow with a pristinely clean white handkerchief, the Don knew that the Brothers Malloy were not in his very home on this very day by chance.

"Even if I have to ride with you like old times, eh?" They all laughed together, the Don louder than the rest.

But the laughter didn't reach the eyes of Gavin or the Don. No one disputed the Don's words or told the older man he was much too infirm to ride dusty trails anymore.

Those two men, even more than Colt or the Don's sons sitting silently by, knew that when the butcher's bill came due, it didn't matter if you were horseback, with both pistols blazing out ahead of you, or dying in a lonely bed, darkness closing in with more familiarity to you than your family and loved ones.

Death came for all men.

Gavin clapped both hands on his dusty pants, and rose with a sigh. Colt rose with his little brother, nodding to the three men who had shared the veranda, and a wonderful respite and meal with them.

Gavin said the last words uttered that night amongst the group of hardened and sunburnt men.

"Well, Don Celso, we better get to it. Morning will come soon enough, and I bet them boys in the Gonzales Gang ain't thinking the Malloy brothers are coming for blood."

Don Celso Baca, the 'Devil Scourge' of New Mexico, along with his two sons, Shooter and Sheriff, watched the brothers leave the veranda and mosey off to find beds warm for the night with a deep and shared sense of relief.

The brothers could never know that the Don and his sons' very lives were to be extinguished the next day, as ransom for return of the Don's two daughters.

Both of his eldest and most beautiful daughters had been kidnapped only days before, and in reparation of men's lives lost amongst the Gonzales Gang, the three remaining Baca men were to be executed the very next morning.

The Don looked over at his two beautiful and barely grown sons and signed the holy cross against his forehead, his heart, and doubled over both shoulders.

He whispered an agonizing prayer under his breath as he did so.

His sons matched the movements and ritual, both without a word, and both in unison.

No, the Don thought as they all sought warm beds that night, soon after, with the women of the large compound cleaning up after what was supposed to be a Last Supper.

It was not by chance that the Malloy's had shown up right when they did, saving the very lives and lineage of a man who owed both brothers more than he could ever pay.

Chapter 25

In the Wild West of the late 1860s, bullets made a much louder statement than spoken words ever could.

And as such, the next morning started out bright, hot, and cloudless, with a thundering amount of the deadly former, and none of the useless latter.

Just as Gavin "Fight Against All Odds" Malloy preferred it.

It was dark, just after 'false dawn,' and Gavin felt great. He was well rested, having slept in the most comfortable bed he'd enjoyed in a very long time the night before, and had a hearty, meat- and tortilla-heavy breakfast before setting out for some killing.

The gunslinger found himself crawling on his belly atop a high hill surrounded by friends and family. They all spied upon the Gonzales Gang, camped out in the valley below.

The sole purpose of being on their bellies on this particular hill overlooking this particular valley was killing. And killing was Gavin's particular specialty.

The valley below held three adobe short houses, with round, exposed wooden beams protruding from the sides. Smoke rose from a chimney atop the middle building.

And all around the three adobe structures, cowboys and banditos were sleeping in bedrolls, horses tied to lead lines nearby. A few dying fires sent tendrils of smoke into the brightening sky.

Gavin and Colt, along with the Don, his two sons, and five of their hired security, focused on the scene below, from the western most end of the short and narrow valley below. Gavin spied out the rest of the valley rim and saw an opportunity to create a killbox. Anytime he and his brother could get the jump on targets, and box them in, numbers counted little for the bad guys.

That was exactly the way Gavin planned out the assault in his mind, and as they crawled backward on their bellies, that's exactly the way he explained the strategy to the group of men he led.

A few moments later, before the roosters even had time to crow, death, hot iron, and blood rained down upon the Gonzales Gang, and a pale horse rode amongst them.

Pancho Perez Gonzales was a generous man. A man of the people. A man of noble girth and strength. And Pancho Perez Gonzales liked the finer things in life.

That's why he always had his men set up his bunk with satin sheets made in Mexico City, and hang hand woven rugs around his sleeping chambers, whenever they made camp. The camp they had made currently, they had been at for a few months, and Pancho Perez Gonzales was getting comfortable.

His father, on the other hand, was a very lean, strict man, who brooked no arguments, took no prisoners, and lived a life of staunch minimalism. The two men were diametrically opposite, except for their bred-in ruthlessness and penchant for hurting others.

Florentine Gonzales was the first to kick Pancho Perez out of his silk-lined bunk, causing a massive bruise to start forming on the younger Gonzales' rear end, and making the young, overweight man hear the gunfire for the first time.

"Get down behind that bunk, and don't make a sound," the senior Gonzales told his son.

Pedro Perez simply nodded a dumb nod and cowered down behind his large bunk. Unlike the rest of the gang, Florentine spoiled his son, and allowed him to bunk inside the adobe building where the cooking fires were.

And now, cowering down behind his large bed, within the shadows of the adobe cooking structure, in the very middle of the Rio Verde Valley, Pedro Perez Gonzales felt real fear for the first time, and could suddenly feel the wetness on the ground under him, where he pissed himself in terror.

Gavin's plan was simple in style, but difficult in execution. A lot would rely on him, and him alone.

But that was just the way he liked it.

He sat atop Mabel and checked his bandolier.

The bandolier was a custom job he had designed and had a saddle-maker build for him. Crisscrossing his body three times, it was made up of six holsters, holding six pistols, and gave him opportunity to spray a lethal rain of iron and fire more than thirty times without reloading. The leather straps holding it all together and tight to his body allowed the carrying of an additional fifty rounds of .45 bullets.

It was heavy, but it had served him well in battle, and in his hunts for multiple outlaws. And wearing it now, having dug it out of his saddle bags, meant that death and ruination was about to be meted out on yet more deserving outlaw bandits.

Looking out over the short, narrow valley, Gavin went back over the plan he had just worked out with the others in his party. He was situated at the head of the valley and would be where any return fire would be directed. He was going to lead the charge, but the other men in his party would make up the pincers on either side, making sure no one got away.

He put the reins between his teeth, pulled out the top two Colt pistols from his bandolier, and kicked Mabel as hard as he could in the ribs. He felt her respond, and kick under him, taking off down the gradual hill toward the sleeping bandits below.

He would have to make the first few shots count, and that would be the signal for the other men gathered to both sides of the camp below to do the same thing he was currently doing.

He and the galloping Mabel reached the sleeping forms of the first set of banditos faster than he had planned, but he made his shots count, firing almost point blank into sleeping forms lying peacefully in sleeping rolls around tamped down fires. He kept firing, both to the left and the right, and soon heard answering shots coming from the pistols and rifles of the rest of his men.

He killed four or five banditos, deep asleep in the pre-dawn light, before the camp knew what had hit them, but the noise of the shots aroused the rest of the Gonzales Gang, and things got hairy real fast after that.

Halfway through the low, scattered fires, and the bodies sleeping around them, Gavin still firing from two pistols, one held in each hand, the thing that always happened during battles happened again to Gavin.

Time slowed down, the world around him starting to move at a snail's pace, yet Gavin moved at the same speed he always had. This routinely happened during the worst of the fighting, and it had saved Gavin's life on several occasions.

As a bandito stood up out of his bedroll, his hat falling behind him, and his right arm lifting, a pistol starting to be aimed at Gavin's heart, Gavin was able to fire off two shots at the man before the man could pull the trigger once.

Another man, to Gavin's right side, lifted a rifle to shoulder height, but Gavin was always a half-second faster, and fired his right pistol at the man, hitting him square in the middle of the forehead.

It happened over and over, and as Gavin mopped up the banditos at the north end of the short valley, he heard the Don, along with Colt, on the left side, and the Don's sons on the right side, meet in the middle, clearing the rest of the sleeping banditos out of the way.

They met near the first of the three adobe buildings, and all pulled pistols, aimed at the man who walked out of the middle structure, his own pistol held to the head of a beautiful Mexican woman.

"Maria," was all the Don said.

The middle-aged man holding the Don's daughter in a death grip, pistol to her head, smiled a half-crooked smile up at the man, yet didn't say a word.

Looking at the stricken face of one of his oldest friends and brothers-in-arms, Gavin knew he needed to do something fast, or this entire situation would be for naught.

Gavin, still watching the events unfolding in his half-time mindset, could almost see what he was going to do a full second before he did it.

Not even saying a word, and not even hardly aiming at all, Gavin Malloy lifted his Colt .45 in his right hand and quick-fired at the man's head.

Gavin hit the leader of the Gonzales Gang, his bullet again finding its mark square in the middle of the forehead, and the man's lifeless body hit the wood decking under him before the previously held woman could even utter a single scream.

It had all happened within a blink of an eye, and in that moment, Gavin Malloy solidified his status as a true legend with the story of how he had killed not only the leader of the Gonzales Gang, but at least other thirty men before they had even fully come awake in the pre-dawn quiet of Central New Mexico Territory.

The story would live on long past the lives of the men who had witnessed it, and Gavin Malloy would go down in Wild West history as the unequivocally fastest and deadliest man in all of the land.

But before all of that could go down in history, the Don, along with his sons and the Malloy brothers, would need to do something about the leader of the Gonzales Gang's chubby and often cruel son, Pedro Perez Gonzales.

And they would have to make an example strong enough out of the rotund, cowardly man, that no one would dare try to come onto or take over the Don's land, ever again.

That's just what the group did, in the most brutal of fashions the Don could devise, in the hot, desert heat of the New Mexico summer.

Chapter 26

Gavin once again sat horseback, watching the Don reunite with his two daughters. Tears streamed down the faces of everyone in the family, and it made Gavin's heart glad that he'd had a hand in doing the right thing.

Well, the right thing until he turned and saw Pedro Perez Gonzales' body staked out on the ground, in the hot sun, being attacked by a mound of angry desert scorpions. The jerking of the fat man's body told Gavin that he was still alive, which was surprising when you thought about the tortures the young man had endured.

Turning back to the Don's smiling face and the looks of relief and happiness on all of his children's faces, Gavin felt better about what they had done. He glanced back toward his own men and saw his big brother Colt light the match and throw it on the pile of bandito bodies.

Well, almost better.

This path they had been set on by General Harrison, for what seemed like months and months now, was doing things to Gavin's soul that he couldn't quite put words to, but the lightheadedness and the sense of ultimate destiny that pervaded his senses most days wouldn't allow him to relax none.

Soon enough, they were back at the comfortable and hospitable home of the Don, with smiles and hugs all around. He hated to think what the Gang would have done with the Don's beautiful daughters, but everyone was home now, and none the worse for wear.

Food and drinks were plentiful, and hearty hugs and smiles greeted the Malloy brothers at every turn. They both felt good about what they had helped accomplish, and without thinking about the carnage and death they had left behind, they allowed themselves to enjoy the festivities until the next morning.

But they had a job to get back to, and conversations to be had with the Don, and plans to make for the next few days. They knew, as did the Don, that they were really only a few days away from the cave systems to the south where Snakebite had made her home.

They would soon ride forward into much more danger than they had beforehand, and careful planning and preparation would be the only thing getting them all out alive.

"Alright, Celso. Let's talk about our next steps," Gavin said to his old friend.

The Don nodded his understanding.

They were once again sitting on the shaded veranda, cool drinks in hand, and bodies sprawled out in comfortable chairs. The atmosphere was still festive and relaxed, but the Malloy's were on edge.

They had a job to do, and sitting around while thinking about it wasn't helping their mental states.

The Malloy's would be facing their hardest test yet in getting Rye Harrison back from Snakebite McGee, and Gavin knew they would need the plan of all plans to come out of that confrontation alive and kicking still.

Rescuing the general's daughter would be paramount, but saving the lives of his men was first on Gavin Malloy's mind that afternoon and into the next day.

As he sat on the veranda, smiling wistfully at the banter between his brother and his oldest friend, Gavin thought back on the only time he'd had a run-in with Snakebite McGee, and the bad taste he had for the outlaw murderer. Going up against her in a real situation worried him beyond belief.

He had been on the trail of a pair of brothers who had murdered their platoon sergeant and had deserted the Union Army.

The trail had brought him here, to the New Mexico Territory, and with the help of his friend and fellow brother in arms, Don Celso, he had hunted the men down to the area of Juarez, on the Texas border.

Border towns in that time were the same as they had always been. Bandits, rogues, and lawbreakers lined the streets and tried to swindle any man to line their own pockets.

The two outlaw brothers, whose names escaped him now, were holed up in an upper floor of a saloon and gambling den.

Gavin and Colt, in full military uniform, and carrying their customary weaponry, entered the saloon area of the creaky structure, only to run full head steam into Snakebite's men.

They'd had no quarrel with Snakebite McGee, as she was a very loud critic and outlier of the War. But the look in her eyes as she sat at a table alone, sipping hard whiskey, as well as the bloodthirsty looks on her men's faces surrounding her, told the Malloy brothers all they needed to know about the outlaw woman.

She was evil incarnate, and Gavin was sure glad they weren't ordered to bring that particular woman to task for her heinous crimes that day, or any day after.

They had finished the job they had been sent to accomplish, having secured the apprehension of the two brothers, and had brought them to justice.

But leaving the gambling den, Gavin Malloy, a legend in his own right by that time, met the eyes of Snakebite McGee, and fear fluttered in his belly for the first time in his life.

He for sure didn't think they would walk away from a fight with that woman unscathed. Nor be able to save Rye from the woman's clutches without someone being seriously hurt, or dying.

And now, they were ordered to do exactly that, and he was afraid for the second time in his very illustrious career as a bounty man and hunter.

The only two feelings of panic and fear he had ever felt were from the same woman.

Gavin felt real trepidation and panic knowing what they were up against, but the unknown worried him even more.

"Gavin," he heard someone say.

Turning his head, he realized that Don Celso had been calling his name for a few seconds. He shook himself out of the memories and faced the task at hand.

"Gavin, tell me now what you need of me," the Don said. "I owe you more than my very life," he said.

Gavin smiled at his old friend.

He was about to burden the Don more than the older man knew, and having deposited enough investments in life and property would be the only way the Don would help the Malloy brothers with their current predicament.

"I need everything you've got, Don. And I need it tomorrow morning."

The look on Gavin Malloy's face shook every man on that veranda that night, but the stoic and seriously terrified look on his face the next morning when over twenty men set out due south worried them all even more.

Chapter 27

As she slept, she dreamed.

Or, more accurately, she thought to herself in the fever dreams, *she saw and heard a great deal about what was going on around her.*

For instance, Rye Harrison saw the entire encounter with the demon and the Entity that had saved Stace Lynn from certain damnation.

Rye was somehow made privy to the information of the lives of both Stace Lynn, the Malloy brothers, and her own part she was to play in all of the unfolding drama.

What she couldn't figure out, and what bothered her slumber and the apparent coma she was in, was just why she was a part of all these goings-on, to begin with.

And so, as she slumbered, slept, remained unconscious, she prayed, and she felt rather than heard answering words and thoughts from Beings she couldn't quite wrap her mind around. What were Ilk's? What was this 'Host' she kept hearing from?

Her comatose nature notwithstanding, she felt like she had a good handle on what was expected of her, at least right up to the point that she would awaken, around about the time the brothers showed up to rescue her.

She also wondered if, upon that awakening, she would remember everything she now knew, or foresaw. She wondered if she would retain the directions and instructions the ArchAngels were giving her, and only her, in her fevered dreams.

For instance, she wondered if she would remember the visions she was given of a future in a mountainous place she had never seen before in her life. She wondered if she would remember that, no matter how bad things got moving forward, that they would all be just fine.

And she wondered finally, her unconsciousness taking her deeper and deeper into realms and existences that she had no way of understanding, if she would remember the future of a universe that made less sense to her than all of it, and what she was shown in her dreams of that place.

A place of reds, blues, yellows, and deepest, endless night. A place of the brightest of lights and the darkest of deep vacuums.

She was shown a universe of emptiness after terrible battles were fought between powers she could no easier understand than the smallest of ants understanding a steam locomotive.

In her dreams, as her body lay suspended in a coma-like trance, her bodily functions ceasing to need releasing, and her mind expanded beyond space and time, she watched as armies of limitless numbers clashed in brightest bursts of energy, and death raining down on planets and solar systems the likes of which she couldn't ever fathom.

Rye Harrison, the daughter of the general, and a young woman of both innocence and means, saw into the very mind of the Almighty, and couldn't understand what it was that she saw. But what she saw frightened her so terribly, she would quake in her boots, had she control over herself.

The dreams reached a fever pitch, and the battles reached a pivotal climax, and what she saw then, the implosion of the very cosmos and all of the planes of existence, made her scream her lungs bloody into the very abyss that was created at the End of All Things.

The sacrifice it took to enact such an ending of everything was the final catalyst that brought her, retching and dizzy, from animated suspension, the scream still lodged in her throat, and her mind buzzing with the after effects of seeing Him… Him who she had seen so many times in her deep dreaming… sacrifice them all for the benefit of the same.

Chapter 28

"You see that cluster of limestone boulders out yonder?" the Mexican scout whispered to Gavin and the Don.

"That's where the cave mouth is. Back behind them rocks," he said.

"The caves cover this whole area of White Sands, all the way down to the border," the man said in broken English mixed with some Spanish.

But both men understood the local man easily.

Gavin nodded to every man around him, and he and the Don, along with Colt, Russ, and twelve of the Don's men, all slithered back on their bellies toward the horse pickets in a copse of trees nearby.

Gavin knew they had to approach this situation carefully. He was all set for an ambush, and knew that the Snakebite lady would have multiple henchmen around, as well as an arsenal of weapons.

They were stepping into her backyard here, and the day could swing the bad way, very quickly.

So Gavin did what Gavin always did in these situations. He gathered his men together, made sure they all knew to stay behind him, and took off running toward the mouth of the large cave deep in the copse of boulders set far back within a large, sandy area.

As they approached the cave mouth, guns drawn, and bullets ready to fly, Gavin was brought up short by the sight of two women, appearing as if by magic from the cave mouth, and both barely recognizable from what he had heard of them both.

And Gavin being brought up short made the men behind him draw up short as well.

All except his brother, Colt.

Colt ran straight into the clearing, with Gavin yelling his name to stop him, but something had ahold of Colt, and as Colt raised both hands holding his twin six-shooters, yelling himself, he let fly with both guns, bullets whizzing toward the two women.

As the women raised their own arms to the air, and the yells from the men entering the clearing lit up the morning with sound and confusion, a bright light burst forth from the cave mouth behind the women, and time itself seemed to stop completely.

And with the blinding light came a voice that shook the heavens and earth, and caused everyone in the vicinity to lose complete control of themselves.

All except the two women, who were at one moment standing at the cave mouth, and the next, lying on the ground, pools of blood spreading under them, the scarlet staining the white sand in an almost criminal way.

Gavin and Colt both found themselves on their knees, Colt several feet in front of his little brother, and dropping his hands, his guns smoking, he looked at the white blouses of the two women, now stained with blood across their chests and stomachs.

But he only saw this scene between the moments of bright lights and huge sounds.

Almost immediately, but lasting eons to all of the people in the clearing, the voice and light died down, and there suddenly stood an old man over the two women's bodies.

Confusion ran like a disease through all those gathered together, and as all of the men of the posse looked on, the old man bent over the two women's bodies, and another light blossomed between them.

All that could be heard in the seconds after the appearance of the old man were the deep, explosive inhalations of both women, and Gavin's voice, sounding far away.

"Archer?" Gavin asked the incredible scene before him.

The old man looked up from the two women still lying at his feet, and smiled a bright, wise grin at all the men, and as he did so, the skies opened up, light shone down on the proceedings, and Colt Malloy fainted right there on his knees, guns falling to the white sand under him.

Chapter 29

Earlier that day, Rye Harrison awoke from what seemed to her a nice long afternoon nap, but to the rest of the world, months had gone by. Her mind was at ease. She felt right as rain after a momentary sense of deepest panic and abject terror.

Stace Lynn Craves didn't understand it at all, but stopped questioning these things after her own transformation, which had been heavy on her mind of late. She didn't have much time to think about *that*, as she needed to figure out what to do with the younger woman now that she was awake.

Rye was moving around, finally questioning where she was out loud, when Stace heard her from the front cave room.

Shoot, Stace thought to herself. *I don't know what to say to this woman.*

And so she did the only thing she knew how to do. She confronted the situation head-on.

Walking back to the cave in which the younger woman had been held unconscious, Stace put a brave smile on her face, and assured herself that the young woman wasn't armed. *Not having a gun,* Stace thought to herself, *I can handle the young woman should she decide to get rowdy.*

Should have called out first, Stace thought to herself, right before she was hit in the face with an empty snake box, knocking her to the ground, making her unable to catch the woman as she ran past Stace lying prone on the sand, blood leaking from her nose.

Stace stumbled into the main room of the cave seconds later, blood and dirt mingling on her face, with spit and anger mixed in, but what she saw as she tried to catch the young woman stopped her dead in her tracks.

The same way it had stopped Rye Harrison, moments earlier.

Archer Wisdom was back, in all of His glory. And when He spoke, the Heavens answered in awe.

"My daughters," he said. "Stand up, please."

Stace was unaware that both she and Rye were on their knees. *When did that happen?* she asked herself.

The two women stood, and watched and waited for direction from the older man who was really God. Rye wore a skeptical, questioning look on her pretty face. Stace knew her own face showed nothing but awe and worship.

Archer smiled at them both.

"How about some breakfast for us and our soon-to-arrive guests?" he asked the women. Both snapped to, as if they had worked together for years, and set about preparing a meal for legions of people. They didn't even question where all of the victuals came from.

The food just *was*.

Within several moments, food was ready, a table was set in the large cave, and Archer Wisdom had his ear aimed toward the cave mouth. He smiled, satisfied that whatever he was listening for had arrived.

He smiled, winked at the two women, and said in a gentle, brook-no-argument tone, "Why don't the two of you walk out and greet our guests?"

As the women did so, finally seeing the men running toward them from the other end of the clearing, one large, lanky, dark-haired man at the lead.

Then bullets flew out, and before anyone knew it, the scene turned into complete chaos.

Neither woman, as they fell to the ground, with bullets riddling their bodies, had disobeyed Archer Wisdom, and as they felt the life leave their young bodies, both knew they never would.

Chapter 30

Rye Harrison found herself in the strangest company, and no one had yet told her how she came to find herself somewhere in the New Mexico territory, surrounded by people she had never met, and no idea how she had gotten there.

And obviously, she had no kind of understanding of what had just transpired, and why her favorite white blouse was covered in her own blood, yet her body had never felt stronger, nor more alive.

She quietly watched the group of people now sitting at a long table, in the middle of a damn cave for God's sake, eating with their hands and laughing together like the most miraculous and ridiculous thing had not just happened!

Which made her glance at the old man sitting at the head of the table again. She couldn't help it. For almost thirty minutes she couldn't take her eyes off the person she now knew to be the Almighty. *Yup*, she thought, *God Himself.*

Wrapping her mind around any part of the day she'd had was damn near impossible, so she just ate along with everyone else, listened in to the conversation and the laughter of the men and the old gentleman at the end of the table, and sat in awe that the shaggy, badly dressed man was God.

Stace Lynn Craves also didn't think too much on what had happened that day, though her eyes were glued not to the Father of All, but to the man who had opened up both of his guns at her and the young woman sitting next to her at the far end of the long lunch table.

Colt saw Stace staring at him, and couldn't quite keep the red out of his own face in shame for his actions. He had no idea what had come over him, had zero idea what had controlled his body or why he had gone against his very nature to run ahead of Gavin and take matters into his own hands.

Gavin, too, was too astounded to speak, and had no idea what was going on now that they had 'rescued' Rye Harrison, but he knew he needed to get her home to her father, badly. He wanted nothing more than to get home to his ranch, now with the fear of the US Army off his back, and worries of the past off of his mind.

And that's when Archer Wisdom cleared his throat, creating silence around the table, and all eyes turned toward him.

"You're all wondering why things worked out the way they did, and what you're going to do now," he stated matter-of-factly.

No one dared move or speak, and a lot of the people around the long, over-burdened table held their breath.

"Well, I'm not going to tell you everything, but I'll tell you some," Archer said.

"You've all surmised by now that I am not an old prospector-turned-preacher from Tascosa," he told the group. Some heads nodded. Most were still.

"And Gavin, at least, has figured out that I'm no Angel either," he said. Eyes shifted to Gavin, who simply nodded and kept his eyes on Archer Wisdom.

"What and who I am is too complicated to explain, but for the time being, put it into your minds that I am the 'God' that you have all heard about and worshiped," he said.

Luckily, no one at the table passed out.

"And the reason I'm here in the cave with you all is that I need your help," Archer said, again, matter-of-factly.

"We are at war, ladies and gentlemen," he told the group. "And as of yet, we don't really know who it is that we are fighting, but we have some guesses."

And at that statement, a light blossomed at the head of the table, and a seven-foot-tall ArchAngel, in full battle armor, holding a weapon shining so bright that it hurt people's eyes, appeared next to Archer Wisdom.

"Gavin, you've already met my son, the ArchAngel Raguel," Archer said by way of introduction.

"To the rest of you, this is one of my children, and a fond lieutenant, Raguel," he said, looking up at the Being standing over him.

Raguel nodded to the men and women sitting at the table, and winked at Gavin. Gavin swallowed noticeably hard.

"You all, on this Earth, and with the help of many more people in this Material Plane, will need to help fight a new war, a war not unlike those many of you have suffered through," he told the men and women at the table.

Every man at the table nodded, expecting nothing less. They had all, to a man, been raised in the caldron of fighting and blood, being soldiers and men born into a time of horrible upheaval.

The women, as well, had experienced their share of war, one being the daughter of a high ranking general, the other fighting for the scraps and leftovers amongst the vultures that followed every army throughout all time and space.

Archer nodded, having heard the thoughts and feelings of all sitting around the long table. Raguel also nodded, understanding what was transpiring. His mind flew forward and backward to times just like this, where similar conversations were had, or were to be had, discussing the same situation in the whole of Creation.

"You all face horrible upheaval and fighting, mere days away," Archer told the group. "And we want to assure you of not only *our* help, but of help from others from far away.'

"It has always been against my very laws to tell mortal humans of the future, and I shall not break that law now,"

Archer said in way of explanation of why he wasn't expounding further.

"But rest assured, whatever you are all to face in the coming trials, you will have the very gates of Heaven opened up, to assure victory," Archer said.

He sat back down, picked up his fork, and ignoring the tall, glowing Angel standing next to him, began to hum to himself and eat the sliced ham and vegetables covering his plate.

And as if a trance had lifted, and clouds parted, every voice around the table began speaking at once, to each other, but mostly toward the head of the table, and were all promptly ignored.

Gavin stayed quiet, though. His eyes wandered back and forth between his older brother, who met his eyes, and the young woman they had vowed to save, who pointedly looked away from his gaze.

Later than night, back amongst the horse pickets and deep within the copse of trees, Gavin looked up from his bedroll, glancing at the stars, and seeing them like it was for the first time again. His mind raced, thoughts bouncing off of each other like hot coals in a banked fire.

Archer Wisdom and the overly large ArchAngel had disappeared almost immediately after the meal, and the day was over almost before they all knew it.

Bedding down assignments had been made quickly and quietly, whispered conversations had stayed low, and everyone in the vicinity was on edge over what was to come.

The Don had agreed with Gavin that he and his men would continue on with the group to see young Rye Harrison home, and there they would part ways.

Both men knew it would be a fitting parting, over on the west coast of the country, as the two had met on the east coast so many years prior.

"Whatever happens," the Don had told Gavin, "I owe you more than my life." Gavin just nodded, still too raw and overwhelmed to do much talking.

"It would do my soul good to help you see that young woman back to her home," the Don had said.

And so, as the night deepened to full dark, and the men bedded down out under the stars and the women did the same inside the cave rooms, peace had descended on the little slice of the world they found themselves in.

And most minds drifted off to an easier sleep then they had thought possible, many thinking of home.

Archer Wisdom and the ArchAngel Raguel looked down on the group of men and women from up high in the Spiritual Plane, the latter retaining his Heavenly Form, and the former finally back in his own Majesty. One smiled; the other frowned.

"I don't like it, Father," Raguel said to the Almighty.

"These few men and women can easier stop the tides from coming and going than to be strong enough to fight against the Horde of darkness coming their way."

The Father of All simply smiled again and reassured his son.

"Hasn't it always been this way?" He asked the ArchAngel.

"Did not Joshua slay mighty armies with few men, or other overwhelming victories earned by a very few?"

"Still, Father, I can't see a victory here," Raguel counter-argued quietly.

The Almighty smiled again, knowingly. He placed an arm around his son, and pulled him in tight.

"Fret not, my son," the Father said. He smiled brighter.

"I still have a plan."

And almost too quiet for the tall ArchAngel to hear, the Creator whispered a last statement to Himself, forming even more questions in Raguel's angelic mind.

"They'll have help. Oh, yes," the Father said, turning away and fading out.

"Plenty of help."

Chapter 31

Fourteen men and two women set out on horseback the next morning, heading straight north, into a colder air blowing downward from the frozen lands for the first time that short fall season.

Pulling his buckskin long coat tighter to himself, Gavin looked forward to being home, in the deep mountains, sitting before the large fireplace hearth at his own home, his brother sitting next to him.

Colt's mind was on similar things, but he needed a drink more than anything that morning they all set out northward. He needed a drink bad. He still could not get out the feeling of something or someone having control of him, forcing him to do things against his very nature.

The Don and his men were all feeling sore in the saddle for the most part, having lost their saddle calluses from the recent lack of long trail rides. But still, spirits were high; they were not herding cattle, which took pressure off minds so early in the morning, and the general conversation was gay and light.

The minds of both women, on the other hand, were full of fear, doubt, and mistrust. Especially for each other.

Stealing glances at each other below wide-brimmed hats, and within deep fur coats, their minds were mostly on each other, and wondering at the situations they found themselves in, seemingly against their very wills.

Rye was looking forward to being home with her aging father, never having seen the man the same way his troops did.

And conversely, Stace found herself wondering just what would become of her after they delivered the young woman back to the home she had stolen her from, and a fear itched within her belly that the woman's father would arrest Stace right there on the spot, sending her straight to the hangman's noose.

She knew she deserved that fate many times over, but it was still a fear that gnawed at her, but which her Father told her not to fret about.

Still, she thought, glancing over at the young woman again, *she couldn't help feeling the fear.*

Gavin's mind was on the trail ahead, and especially what the man who he had known as Archer Wisdom had told him. War was coming. A war unlike anything the men had ever seen. A war, battles without number forthcoming, that would put Gavin and his men to the ultimate test, whatever that was.

His mind was on intense alertness, waiting for dark things to jump out from every bush and boulder they rode around. His nerves were strung high, and he twitched at every sound and smell around him.

He couldn't keep up this level of alertness, he knew, but still, like others in the group, he couldn't help feeling the way he did, all based on the words of the man he had known for years, and had had no idea was really the Almighty in disguise.

It made sense though, he thought to himself, looking back on his interactions with the older man down through the years.

Archer Wisdom had always lived up to his surname.

Considering the advice, directions, and forgiveness the old man had given to Gavin's actions and needs during the War of the States made Gavin see what he had missed before.

Archer Wisdom had never been what he seemed. His words and actions were contrary to anyone else Gavin knew, and that made Gavin accept and fully embrace that he was being Watched and directed by the Almighty and His Angels.

That fact alone gave some small peace to Gavin's mind, but still it raced with alertness and fear.

His racing thoughts and quick glances around every hidden hollow and tree were suddenly interrupted by a single question, spoken in a small, husky voice, from behind him and to his right.

The question on the air surprised him in its words, but even more so from its tone.

"You fought for my father in the War, didn't you?" Rye Harrison asked Gavin Malloy. "I know the haunted look of a soldier who has seen hell," she said.

Deep on the trail north, taking her home, and back to a life far from anything Gavin himself knew, Rye had spoken the first words she had ever said to her rescuer with that question.

For several quiet moments he did not know how to answer her at all.

And when he finally did answer, doing so opened up a flood of memories and words that surprised him in their intensity and thoroughness, through the rest of that day, and for more than one day after.

"Yes and no," he told her unabashedly.

"I was under his command, but I fought my own war, and I fought it the only way I knew how," he said.

"My way."

There was a long pause from her side, which made him glance back at where she sat – *extremely able and capable*, he thought fleetingly – and he watched as the confusion on her face turned to curiosity.

"You're going to have to explain that one to me," she said, finally, in reply.

She kicked her own horse gently, moving beside Gavin on the trail. Equally keeping pace with him and Mabel.

And to his own confusion and curiosity at the level of comfort he had doing so, he did exactly what she asked.

He explained everything to the young woman with the intense blue eyes, and the open heart of an innocent, who rode next to him, all the way to where they had to be getting to.

Chapter 32

Wandering north and then west through New Mexico Territory and finally into southern Utah, the first chill of the winter season descended upon the tired, dusty group of men and women.

As scattered snowflakes fell, blowing and twisting in the chill air, the group traveled close through deep canyons and a harsh red landscape meant to keep folks out rather than invite them in.

The cold pressed in deep, making everything else they had worried about seem trivial.

Gavin's mind went to the trail ahead, as it did most days, and stayed there. He was a forward thinker, and he knew it. He had found the same in the young woman who still rode next to him, her own buckskins pulled close. Lucky finding those, he thought fleetingly, as they had refitted in New Mexico before heading north.

He was taken aback by Rye's strength, and had wrongly figured her for a soft, spoiled woman of means, but her hardiness on the trail and the many times she had proven how capable she was, surprised everyone, including him.

She had explained her strength and knowledge of trail riding with a simple shrug and a tossed away statement.

"I grew up in Army camps with Dad. But it was really my mother who taught me how to be strong in a world controlled by men," she had told him.

"Mom was a frontier woman like no one you have ever met, Gavin," she went on, on the day he had asked.

"She was tough. And she made sure her only daughter was just as tough," Rye had told him.

Their conversations were light and far apart, but even so, Gavin felt himself opening up. He didn't tell her the worst of it; how could he? But what he had told her and how she had absorbed and responded positively to, told him volumes about her character and grit.

He was growing to admire her greatly, which was doubly dangerous out in the open wilds. An admiration could turn down right disastrous should trouble spring up, and his instincts went to covering the young woman first.

But it couldn't be helped, and as the miles passed away behind the steps of the dozen or more horses they traveled with, his respect for the young woman grew.

The snow was picking up a bit as they passed into the Painted Desert area of southern Utah Territory, and Gavin knew that the tribes of natives a little further north would migrate down south into the area they were riding through.

The Ute and the Uintah tribes were fierce fighters, and he had no desire to meet any of them as they passed through the large, open yet mountainous regions they still had to travel.

"Hold up, y'all. Hold up," Gavin told the group.

He was still considered the leader of the band, even though the Don had outranked him in almost every way a man could. The Don was gracious to the Malloy brothers, and frankly, Gavin knew, the older man was tired of leading.

"Let's find us a nice warm cave or arroyo to hole up in. This snowstorm will pass quickly," he told the men and two women.

Everyone nodded their understanding, and looking toward a warm fire and some hot grub, started spreading out looking for suitable shelter and dry firewood. The area offered plenty of both.

Soon, one of the Don's men shouted a loud 'whoo-hoo,' and everyone moved their tired horses toward the man. He had found a deep cave at the base of a tall spire of rock, gaily painted by the Lord Almighty in every color of the russet rainbow. Gavin nodded his approval and dismounted.

"We have to take watching the horses in shifts. They can't fit in the cave, and the tribes hereabout want nothing but to steal the horseflesh," he told his band.

Heads nodded understanding, and lots were silently cast to see who would stand first watch.

It wasn't a bad job, sitting watch. But it could get lonesome, and with the snow starting to pick up, it would be uncomfortable. Gavin would make sure whoever was standing watch had plenty of blankets, a clean, well-kept shotgun, and the first bowl of soup from Colt's supper fixins.

Colt and Stace would do the cooking together, as they had the entire trip north. Gavin watched the pair set out stores and start up the fire with a cautious eye. He still didn't know what to make of the woman who seemed to be the exact opposite of everything he had ever heard about her. But Archer Wisdom told him to put his trust in the woman, and he meant to honor that promise.

It still made him jumpy, though. The woman had the reputation of being the worst of the worst in murderous banditry, and the only thing that had kept the Malloy brothers off her trail was that she was a woman, and had been smart enough to not disturb the Union Army.

But now, his hackles rose watching the ease with which his brother and the outlaw woman got on. It wasn't that he wasn't happy that Colt and Snakebite were like two peas in a pod, he just couldn't meld what he knew about both people, his brother more than the young woman, into what he was seeing before him.

And as always, as they set up camp, it wasn't Colt and Snakebite that grabbed his attention and distracted him in that moment, his thoughts of them both notwithstanding.

It was Rye Harrison who made him feel uncharacteristically out of sorts.

Soon enough, just to clear his head, he took two bowls of hot beef and vegetable stew out to the young man who had lost the draw and stood first watch.

Gavin saw that it was the Don's youngest son, his own adopted godson, Sheriff, sitting atop the canyon wall, rifle slung across his lap, heavy Mexican blankets wrapping his shoulders tightly.

Handing the bowl to the young man, Gavin took a seat next to him. They both set to eating the hot soup before it could grow cold in the increasing winter storm.

Soon, both men were finished eating with no words spoken between them. But Gavin handed his bowl to the much younger man, and told him in a tone that brooked no argument to seek out his bedroll.

Sheriff nodded his understanding, having learned long ago to not question his elders, and scampered off the canyon wall, moving down to find rest and heat in the comfortable cave the men had found.

Gavin scooted his butt to get a comfortable position and set about watching the land around them, while focusing on his own thoughts for the first time in their rush north.

This was a familiar exercise he needed often, but which circumstances often prevented him from achieving.

Sorting his thoughts, away from other people, and being able to put things in line in his own thinking was paramount in the days to come. Since everyone looked to him to get the young woman, Rye Harrison, back home safely, and also to prevail against whatever was coming their way, the warning from Archer Wisdom still loud in his mind, he needed his wits in a clean, straight line.

And so, as the flakes of snow grew larger, the wind calmed, and the land around him transformed into clean, white blanket-covered hills and valleys, spires and desert beauty, his mind worked over every bit of information since he and Colt had received the letter back on the ranch, what seemed like a lifetime before.

He organized, sorted, and filed away things he didn't quite understand, and focused on the things that he did. He took the presence of the ArchAngels and the Father as a matter of course. Having grown up with a determined mother who had taught both her sons about faith and the Lord, it was just a matter of the invisible coming visible, and Gavin could understand that.

The young woman having been kidnapped by Snakebite and her men, on the other hand, he couldn't quite figure, so he filed it away for another day. As did the question he had about those same men. Where had they gone? Did they just disappear on the woman, or did Archer somehow get rid of them himself?

It was a question he didn't want to ask the young woman, and at the end of things, he knew it didn't much matter what happened to the group of roughnecks she had often been seen with. If they weren't right in front of Gavin, shooting at him, or those he cared about, he just as rather let the questions go.

His way of organizing his thoughts was to focus and find peace in what he could handle, and put away things most men would chew over for days.

He had always known he never had that kind of time to mull over things he couldn't understand or control anyway.

And soon enough, his hat weighted down with powdery white snow, and the land around him darkening into the baleful glow of winter wonder, Gavin found his thoughts, at least, at peace, and he could finally breathe a deep sigh of relief, settling in for whatever lay ahead.

That's when he heard scattering stone behind him, and knew it was her, coming to check up on him, as she had done a few times on the ride north. Her footsteps were light, but he knew them, and a slight perfume, her smell, preceded her. That knowledge, mixed with his senses being attuned to her, made him settle down deep within himself, and a burgeoning… something… arose deep in his chest and abdomen.

The deepening darkness was lit up by the bright white snow, and the stillness in the falling flakes made sounds muffled yet travel far at the same time. The eeriness of the evening was made tolerable with the knowledge and feelings of the young woman's attention and care of Gavin Malloy.

It was one of the things he had put away the understanding of, for another day.

And as she settled in next to him, her own heavy blanket folded neatly under her, he looked over at her face and wondered at why he had never noticed just how beautiful she was, with her cheeks rosy, red from the cold and the exertion of the climb up to the top of the canyon wall.

Or the way her hair swept constantly into her eyes making his heart sing for the deep sigh he barely kept in.

She looked over at him and as their eyes met, his nice, orderly thoughts and the deep peace within his mind almost lost all order and scattered again. Only with an iron willpower and control over himself that he had learned early in life could he assure he kept his wits about him.

He felt the young woman sitting next to him, who now looked out over the white vista of the beautiful scenery about them, had no such need to control herself, having that built-in control all women seemed to possess.

The quiet between them grew as comfortable as the quiet around them, and the snows settled in deep, the air grew even dryer and quieter, and soon enough, with the darkness closing in, peace settled around the couple like a comfortable old blanket on tired bones.

Her gloved hand found his in the darkness, and with no words needing to be said between them, an understanding arose, and a future was finally decided.

A future decided not only in the world around them, but in the Heavenly Realms above, where a Host looked down on a scene that brought a balm of quiet to many angelic auras.

Chapter 33

Lying in her bedroll next to Stace Craves later that night, Rye Harrison thought about the rough man she had just joined her fate to. And she thought back to the reasons why she knew deep in her heart that she was going to do so. It had begun the moment she saw him and his men running toward the cave, into an unknown outcome, just to save her.

She knew what that had taken, as her father had explained so much to her about military tactics and what he called 'charging the breech.' And she knew what type of man it took to do just that for a complete stranger.

Oh, Gavin had waved it off, explaining how he and his brother were trying to save their own lives in the exchange for hers. However, she knew the truth of her father well. He wasn't a monster or an evil man.

Her father was the most dedicated and noble man she knew, and she also knew that he wouldn't have sent the Malloy brothers after his only daughter without a full battalion of soldiers unless there was something to these two men.

And it was that 'something' that had drawn her to Gavin Malloy. She fell into a peaceful sleep, a smile on her lips, thinking about the future. And what she, herself, saw in Gavin Malloy.

Lying next to Rye Harrison, eyes still open in the darkness of the still cave, snow falling outside muffling the world, Stace Lynn Craves thought only of the past.

Flashing scenes of what she had done with most of her life passed before her mind's eye, in full, vivid color and detail. Her stomach cramped up at the shame and guilt, and tears sprang from her eyes, blurring the darkness, making it as muffled as the world outside their shelter.

Then, like a bolt of lightning, her mind was taken over, and a new image flashed before her eyes, almost projected onto the dark cave wall beside her. The older Malloy brother.

Colt.

She found a kindred spirit in the man. She could see it in his eyes, and his almost hidden nips from a whiskey flask as they had ridden north.

The day he had rode up beside her, an apology on his lips about shooting her three times in the stomach and chest, made her smile, forgetting the tears.

No one had ever apologized to her in her entire life.

It was a new experience that she had casually brushed away out loud to the skinny, rugged man. But inward, her middle had quaked, almost unseating her from the saddle.

She could barely control a smile all that day.

The man had then ridden his sleek stud horse next to her the rest of the trip into the Badlands. Or what some called the Painted Desert. In her circle of work, it would always be known as the Badlands. All the way north to damn near the Canadian border, the Badlands were where you did not want to get caught out in the open, alone.

She knew all too well the rough banditry, and the dangerous natives who spoke only in a language of violence, hereabouts.

It worried her, but as she looked back down the past and considered the small bits and pieces she had heard of the Malloy brothers mixed with what she saw in them every day of the trip north and west, she didn't worry as much as she would have in the past.

And that, too, was a novel experience. To feel safe in the steady hands of two men who had as dark a past as she.

Stace Craves fell into a fitful sleep thinking of all the ways her own life had changed in such a short time, and even more so, of the man who now occupied more of her thoughts than she would outwardly admit to, but which inwardly warmed her heart.

The next morning dawned bright and calm.

Snow covered the scrub bushes and rock formation around the group of cowboys. The muffled, heavy air pressed in, cold, crisp, but clear and clean.

Gavin stepped out of the temporary shelter and breathed in deep, letting the cold, clean air wash away any trepidation and fear, and to say a quick prayer to the heavens for the miracle and new love that had come into his life, and which he knew, deep down, he didn't deserve.

And that made him think of Rye's father, the general, and what he, himself, was going to do about the older man.

Gavin told himself that he would worry about that when he had to, as he stomped ice away from a small creek next to the rock outcropping so that the horses could drink.

Gavin mentally went over what the group would do today, and whether they should push onward, risking limb and hoof to unseen dangers under the couple of inches of snow that had fallen overnight.

They needed to take stock of what supplies they had, and what they would need to either find and gather, or requisition at the next town.

On the way north, the large group had made two stops for re-supplying. One was at the Don't own home in Santa Rosa, and then again in Santa Fe, New Mexico Territory, where a very large Army depot stood, and from which the group had been able to get just about everything they could think of for the trip to the west coast, and even some things that they may not have needed, but which was nice to have anyway.

And so, clean thoughts and clean air in his lungs, Gavin set about securing the saddle bags, riggings, and lead lines of the horses while he let the men sleep in.

He looked up to see a small line of smoke above their temporary shelter which told him someone was making breakfast, and he assumed either Colt or one of the women was awake at least.

That sight made his mind go back to Rye Harrison, and their unspoken commitment the night before.

His feet were getting cold in his rough boots, and his hands were reddening up until he put his riding gloves over his chapped skin, but he didn't want to set right back into the warmth of the cave just yet.

He needed to take the time to wrap his mind around a nagging thought that he couldn't quite shake, and it would do no one, especially Rye Harrison, any good until he got his head over it.

That fact was simple. His past, and the sins he had committed in the name of just being good at it, made it impossible for him to accept the woman's love.

He didn't deserve a shred of comfort or softness, and he knew it.

If he didn't get his mind around this conundrum, he and Rye Harrison would just have had a single evening of shared excitement over a future that would never happen, and he would deliver her to her father posthaste.

He needed to find forgiveness in himself before he could let that beautiful woman love him completely. He knew that, and he knew that she knew it as well. It was in the last glance she had given him the night before, as she moved back down to the cave, to a warm bed and, he hoped, warm dreams.

He decided to take a walk around the desert landscape they found themselves in this morning, and hope to all that he could get his mind right. And if he couldn't, then he hoped at least to make some small dent in decision making of what lay ahead.

Gavin Malloy's boots crunched in the snow, making sounds like walking on dead, dry leaves as he walked away from his group of men, toward the west and a tall mountain he saw in the distance.

The early morning air was clear and crisp, and he pulled his dust popper buckskin jacket closer to his neck. It was quite cold in the clear morning, but that clarity and crispness made the eye able to see farther than most days.

And that mountain in the distance, whatever its name, wouldn't have been visible any other way, this far out.

Moving around still-green mesquite trees and tall yucca, he kept on walking, his mind working a million miles a minute to the issues as he saw them.

Forgotten for the moment were the impending battles and hardships Archer Wisdom had told him would come in the future, and instead, Gavin's mind wandered back down the miles and miles of memories of the past.

The violence, the steady, everyday stress and strain of being on alert, the deaths, the hunting. It all came rushing back to this mind and made his knees weak with the onslaught.

He walked and walked as he pondered the past, the images coming like a moving picture, one of those movie things he had heard about playing in San Fransisco and out east, to New York City.

The blood, the gun fights, pulling wanted men out of every kind of hidey hole they could find. The fear on their faces, and the pain in their eyes as they saw the Malloy brothers on their doorsteps.

The cries of children, the pleadings of wives. The begging of condemned men, and the pleas to spare life. Of which Gavin Malloy had never listened to.

What kind of monster of a man he had been, and what kind of a woman would ever love a man like him? The question reverberated around his mind, over and over, the words running into each other until it became one long, unrecognized sound in his head. A screaming sound, buzzing gnats eating at swollen, dead faces, the line of the question became overbearing.

He didn't see where he was walking, he didn't hear anything around him, just the guttural, screaming noise of the conjoined words, berating him, tearing him apart, becoming one long sound of torturous guilt and condemnation.

The scream turned outward; he could feel his throat pick up the sound, and the echoing guilt from the rock walls around him, the gully canyon he found himself in, slamming the sounds of his screams back to him, compounding the condemnation.

He couldn't hold in the sound. He had no control of himself or the memories circling his mind. Gavin had no choice but to watch the past overload him with its blood, its horror, and the death that stained his own hands crimson.

Screams, sounds, battles, loud, agonizing noise overwhelmed his senses, and he had no way of seeing the world around him, or the clean, bright future he hoped for.

All he could see and hear was the guilt.

A crescendo of sounds took away all sight, sound, and feeling from Gavin Malloy. He was on his knees in the snow, deep in a crevasse in the earth, and he saw and felt none of it.

Until a gentle hand laid on his shoulder, love radiating from it, brought all the sounds and sights of the present rushing back in, and he looked up into the face of his Redeemer.

Archer Wisdom stood next to Gavin where he knelt on the hard, rocky ground, his breeches growing wet from the snow, and tears, snot, and spit starting to freeze in his beard and on his face.

Archer only smiled down on Gavin, allowing the man's senses to return to him, and allowing Gavin to look around at where he found himself.

And where he found himself was a sight he couldn't comprehend, like his surroundings didn't belong on the earth at all.

A high, overhead arching bridge of stone was the first thing he saw, bigger than anything he had ever seen, and the fact that he and Archer stood in the shadow of the giant arch, deep in a stone-walled canyon, the ground he thought he was walking on high overhead, began to make him feel vulnerable again.

Like an exposed nerve, Gavin's thoughts and emotions threatened to explode once again.

Finally, Archer Wisdom spoke, and the torture and guilt that had just been the only things Gavin could see or feel dissipated on the air, like a shimmering heat mirage on the hottest of summer days.

"That's about enough of that, I think," Archer said.

And the heavens opened up, the day brightened, and Gavin's heart felt a peace he had not known since he was a very small boy, sitting in his father's lap, staring into the dancing happiness of a family fire, the night's dinner cooking atop it.

"Yup," Archer said down at the man, a man who was one of his favored children. A man who would go on to be instrumental to so much more on the cosmic and existence level than anyone else could fathom.

"That's about enough of that, my son."

To Gavin Malloy's surprise, it was enough.

More than enough.

Chapter 34

"Every choice you make, every step you take, and every thought you have, affects and dictates your entire life, and afterlife," Archer explained.

"Both good and bad," he said.

Gavin just nodded. He knew the Almighty disguised as an old man he had known for years was right.

"But at any given moment, new thoughts, experiences, and solutions can be experienced, and your entire future can change. In a single moment, Gavin," Archer said.

"And that's what's done here. You felt the overwhelming shame, guilt, and power of the mistakes and evils you experienced and created in your past, and not wanting it a part of who you want to be, you called the Observers down, and thus, received absolution. You received redemption."

It made sense to Gavin, however painful it had been. He knew the words from the Father were correct. He had just felt the lifting up and off of the weight of his past, and he was ready to be the man that Rye, and himself, needed him to be.

"And it happened right here, at one of the Nodes of this world, the place where the veil wears a bit thin, and holiness can be mistaken for uniqueness," Archer said, looking up at the large, overarching stone bridge above them both.

"I love this place in particular," he said to no one.

The two men both breathed in deep of the cold, winter air. It was cleansing in itself, and Gavin wondered fleetingly if the Almighty Himself needed a bit of cleansing once in a while.

It was a sacrilegious thought, but wasn't he himself made in the Almighty's image? And if he just had need of cleansing from the experiences he had, surely the Father needed a place to go and wash His own Spirit clean of what He saw in Creation.

Archer chuckled at Gavin's thoughts, making Gavin blush.

"No, you're right as rain, Gavin Malloy," Archer said, his kind, wizened face smiling brightly.

"I am in constant need of solitude and what you would call a re-setting," the old man finished.

After those words, the two men sat under the shadow of the tall land bridge for some time, allowing the cold and the

201

presence of the Almighty wash over and around the cold canyon walls, making them both a bit warmer.

"Now, Gavin, I must be elsewhere, but I want to prepare you for what's to come tomorrow," Archer said, a grave look taking over the serene calmness of a second before.

"What we spoke about in the cave in New Mexico is upon us all, and it's pivotal that you know what to expect," Archer said.

"It's not my way to instruct and give information like this, my son, but this attack is of utmost importance, and if we are not successful here, I'm afraid the entire thing could come crashing down," the Father of the Universe told the long, thin cowboy.

"Now," he said to the suddenly nervous man sitting next to him in the shadows of the land bridge, the sun rising high overhead, "we have just enough time for a story, and for you to get back to your men, and Rye Harrison, to prepare them," Archer Wisdom said.

"So, about, oh, I reckon twenty-two hundred years or so ago, a very large Persian army, on the other side of this world, attacked a much smaller set of countries and principalities," Archer said. Gavin hung on every word.

"One of the smallest yet fiercest countries in the city states was called Sparta," Archer said, looking over at Gavin. Gavin nodded. His father had told him this story. But he was sure that the Almighty would know it a little more… personally.

"The king of Sparta was named Leonidas, and he was truly a lion of a man," Archer told Gavin.

"The idea was, if they could stop the advance of the much larger Persian army at two places, one on land, the other on the sea, the smaller city states could band together like they had done against the Persian emperor's father, many years before," he said.

"King Leonidas took three hundred of his own men, and only about a thousand of the men from other, smaller countries, to hold the land route at a place called Thermopylae.

"As the King led his men in a week of harsh fighting, holding back an army ten times the size of his own, we watched what you humans could inflict on each other. It was ghastly, and brutal," Archer said with sadness in his tone.

"The night before the last day of the battle, with most of his men dead, or having been sent away, I visited Leonidas in his tents. I spoke to him, just as I'm speaking to you now." Archer looked over at Gavin Malloy again.

"We observe everything, Gavin. My children and I see all, and take it upon us a responsibility to assure certain outcomes, based on the Laws that I established when I created this Universe," Archer said.

His tone was as serious as Gavin had ever heard. The thought that he was speaking to the Almighty Himself was not lost on the man, and his mind reeled, and his head became light just thinking of it.

Archer's next words jolted him back to the present.

"I told Leonidas, that night, what I'm about to tell you," Archer said.

"Tomorrow, your entire life is going to end, Gavin Malloy. Everything you have ever known will be what we call *finite*."

Archer Wisdom looked down at the gangly cowboy with a somber, severe face.

"But the purposes behind your life, the very reason you were born, will have been revealed, completed, and acted upon, thus assuring this road show we call existence carries on," Archer said.

Gavin gulped loudly. He assumed what any man would assume, he thought. He could feel his body start to shake in the cold morning air.

God Almighty had just revealed to him that he would die the next day.

Chapter 35

Colt Malloy stomped his boots loudly, dislodging the snow built up under his heels. He sure was glad that he and Gavin had ridden so many trails together, through all kinds of weather and environments.

Thinking ahead, they had stocked themselves well, including thick, wool, Army-issue socks.

A man could die a nasty death without good socks, he knew.

Pulling the cinch strap on his saddle as tightly as he could, his stud stallion looked back at him with a comical, exasperated air about him. Colt smiled at the tall roan, finished looping the strap through the buckle, and patted the old boy on his thick neck and front haunches.

Colt scratched the tall horse where he knew he liked it best. Right between the front flanks, deep within the muscular chest of the old horse.

"Need a good brushing, don't you, old man?" Colt asked the tall horse.

Snorting in the cold air, his breath clouding in front of him, the horse caught the barely concealed fear in Colt's middle, and side stepped a bit. Colt reassured the roan with a gentle hand and whispered promises of good things to come.

A man and his horse had a stronger bond than most, Colt thought to himself, finishing up laying saddle bags on the stallion's rear flanks, and holstering his newly-oiled Golden Boy rifle.

A bond stronger than almost any, except family, and a love interest.

Colt had his thoughts on other things this early morning, and as if he summoned them himself, his brother and Stace Lynn Craves walked out of the sheltering cave together.

They were talking in hush whispers, and Colt felt a stirring of jealously bend his heart a bit, but he knew his brother had eyes for the general's daughter, which brought on a whole slew of feelings, none of them good.

So he put the jealous feelings aside easily, and thought of the trail further north and west. The trepidation of the unknown future lay a bit heavier than the petty jealously, and those were the emotions his horse had caught scent of.

They had to rid themselves of the young woman, so as to continue on with living the way they wanted to. Colt had already figured Stace Lynn into that life, but he didn't know how to brook the subject to Gavin.

Another conversation for another day, he mused as he watched his brother cinch up Mabel, his conversation with Snakebite finished for the moment.

Colt wondered briefly what that had been about.

Gavin's face showed deep concern this fair, bright morning, and what Colt would call fear, if he didn't know Gavin better than that.

Horses saddled, every firearm and rifle in the group oiled and loaded, ammo belts slung across chests, and as much preparation done the day before as could be, the group set out north by west, toward a large mountain growing ever larger in the distance.

He had heard the name of the mountain from some of the trail cowboys employed by the Don. It was called *Un-chu'-ka-ret* by the local Indian tribes, though Colt Malloy figured it would get a white man's name before too long.

This whole part of the world, what others called the Badlands, was getting more and more attention from the folks out east.

Colt's mind went back to his brother, and the puzzle of what was going on in the head of the younger man.

Gavin had come back from a long walk the day before, just in time for a lunch of beans and cornbread, with a look of absolute horror on his face. He had locked eyes with Colt, promising further details of what bothered him, but that conversation had still not come.

Colt Malloy knew his brother well. And if something could shake the man as much as he seemed to be shaken, maybe Colt didn't want to know what his little brother knew.

Melting snow crunching under their horses' hooves, the runoff of a warming day making muddy prints across the painted desert, the group made good time toward a series of canyons and valleys in the southern-most section of the Ute Reservation lands, and just north of the Navajo range.

Rocky formations appeared out of the bright blue day, and Colt happily spied the land bridges his brother had described to many the day before. They lay off to the south, but still discernible in the morning sunlight glinting off the melting snow.

They had all gone searching for them the afternoon last, and had found four in an area of a few miles. The tall, over-arching land bridges, high overhead of deep canyon floors, were awe inspiring and beautiful. A hum of energy, a vibration of peace, seemed to emanate from each bridge.

Riding slowly but surely north and west into a deep, broad valley beyond the stone arches, the day was looking better and better to Colt Malloy, who happily followed his brother into whatever future awaited them, knowing that they had done the job they were tasked with, and as soon as they rid themselves of the young Rye Harrison, the quicker they could get on back to Montana, and a snowy, lazy winter rest.

Colt had his mind on whiskey, rest, their childhood home, a possible future with Stace Lynn Craves, and the comfort of a warm fire in their hearth, and good food in his belly. The mixture of old memories with future hopes made the spindly, rough-skinned man feel happy feelings for the first time in a long time.

Looking ahead at the back of his little brother, who led the caravan of a dozen good fighting men, and two women, he smiled, knowing that he and Gavin would grow old together, a home promised far away but growing closer every day, and long hot summers working their own land, profits coming from their own sweat. Colt smiled a shy smile and felt his stallion below him catch the positive feelings, almost leaping with heightened joy.

Colt patted the stallion lovingly on the side of his long neck, nearly bending over to do so.

As he rose up tall in the saddle, glad that the horse could feel his happiness, two things happened simultaneously.

His stallion buckled up, nearly unseating Colt, as the large mountain several miles ahead of them exploded in a bright light, and a sound like dozens of the largest twisters ever imagined came from behind the group, back where the stone arches lay over deep canyon walls.

Not knowing where to look, or what exactly he was looking at, Colt first saw hundreds and then thousands of large, dark shapes flying from the exploded top of the mountain to the west, and could feel the heat of thousands of similar, but brighter, larger shapes fly from the arches behind them.

The group of fourteen men and two women found themselves caught between a tornado and a volcano, and didn't know what the hell to do.

Horses scattered, men clinging on for dear life, and the circling groups of shapes, dark against light, gathered high overhead, flashes of lightning beating down on the earth around the group.

And that's when Gavin started yelling to the group, giving instructions like he had known this nightmare was coming, and Colt suddenly realized that his little brother had, indeed, known what was coming.

Colt skinned both his six shooters, as did all the men around them, and the last thing he thought for a very long time was that at least that mystery could be put to rest. Bullets flew from the group up at the dark things coming closer and closer, and the men and two women met them with everything they had.

Colt thought back to his brother during the melee.

Gavin had known what was to come today, and Colt felt both better for knowing that, and deep, unresisting fear that he had no idea what the hell that meant.

Or what was about to happen next.

Chapter 36

From as far away to the west as San Fransisco, south
to the great cattle towns of deep cowboy country Texas, and
east to the dusty towns of the Kansas plains, a storm rose up
from the Badlands, unlike anything anyone had seen or heard.

But see it and hear it now, they did.

An eerie green light emanated from the mountain top
to the west, and as Gavin looked at it, wondering what it was
he was seeing, dark black arrows rained down around him and
his men, each one sizzling, a small puff of smoke being

released as it hit the snow and dirt beneath their horses' hooves.

"Cover! Get to cover!" he yelled to the men and women around him.

Luckily, there was plenty to be had in the canyon lands around them. Deep crevices, lined in limestone and sandstone, dotted the land they had ridden through all morning.

How he didn't lose a man in the first confusing moments of the attack was beyond him, but as the group sought cover in a deep canyon, he turned his thoughts to what he saw ahead.

A large land bridge came into view in front of them, and they made for it before the dark things dotting the blue sky could reach them.

But as the group of cowboys and two women reached the bridge, the rocky ground under it covered in snow, gravel, and sand, it lit up, the bridge becoming so bright the horses all reared up on their hindlegs at the sight.

Then a magical sound like tinkling glass, a thousand times louder than normal, burst from the light, and a row of armored Beings, feet taller than the tallest man, stood all in a row.

They gleamed like a colorful rainbow, movement so awesome a human eye couldn't follow.

Gavin tried to count the rows of ArchAngels but gave up as they flew as one up into the bright blue sky, to wreak havoc upon the darkness found there.

All eyes to the skies as flashes of light, peals of thunder, and a barrage of sounds meant that no one saw the single, unassuming man step out of the brightness of the landbridge behind the Angels.

A clearing of a throat made Gavin look back over at the bridge, seeing the middle-aged man standing there holding a box. A glowing, metallic box.

As the light of the bridge faded away, and the sounds of the battles overhead moved away toward the mountainous region to the west, Gavin walked Mabel up to the man standing in the sand beneath the now back-to-normal bridge of stone overhead.

The man, simply dressed, but in clothing that Gavin couldn't quite recognize, looked up at him and smiled a smile with dazzling white teeth.

"Hello there," the man said in a bright, happy tone. He had an accent from back east, but Gavin couldn't quite place where back east he had come from.

Gavin Malloy was put instantly at ease by the man, but he couldn't say why. The man had appeared the way the small yet awe-inspiring ArchAngel army had, and Gavin could only surmise that he had come from the same place.

"I've brought you something," the man said, lifting up the metal box in his hands. It seemed heavy, but the man didn't have a problem lifting it up almost chest-high.

Gavin interrupted the man. He had so many questions.

"Who are you?" Gavin asked. "Archer didn't tell me about no man coming," he said down at the still-smiling man.

The man smiled brighter and put the heavy metal box on the ground. When he raised back up, he wiped his hands on his pants, pants made from a material Gavin had never seen. It was coarse and heavy and blue.

The man walked over to Mabel, walking alongside her, and put a hand on her neck in a kind, gentle manner. He moved up to Gavin's right, and extended his hand.

Gavin bent down low in the saddle as all the men and women around him watched. He and the newcomer shook hands, and Gavin was surprised at the strength of the man's grip.

"Well met, Gavin Malloy," the man said. Gavin surmised they were of an approximate age.

"My name is Benjamin Reeves. And I'm what you'd call a Storyteller," the man told Gavin. "You can call me Ben, though. Everyone does."

The name didn't mean anything to the rangy cowboy, but that didn't seem to bother Benjamin Reeves. Their hands parted ways, and Ben walked back over to the box sitting in the dirt.

As he approached the box, he reached down and opened a lid with no hinges. Sitting inside was a massive mound of perfectly made silver bullets. Of several calibers.

"My wife sent me here with these. Thought you could use them," Ben Reeves said.

"They are bullets for your guns. None of them will jam up or misfire on you. But they are made from a material that can kill those things out there. And trust me, guys," Ben told Gavin and the group, "you'll want to kill as many of them as you can."

The man who had introduced himself as Benjamin Reeves walked back over to Gavin where he still sat saddle on the back of his mare, Mabel.

Ben patted the horse on the neck again, Mabel enjoying the man's attention. He smiled up at Gavin again, and put the tautly-pulled cowboy at ease.

"We've been fighting this enemy for eons, Gavin Malloy," he told him soberly.

"And we could really use your help. The Father tells us that you're someone special, and we needed to give you a hand on what He has asked you to do here today," Ben said.

"My wife and I were given the same help, and we in turn have spent more time than I can explain returning the favor," he said.

Gavin still couldn't find his voice. Too many thoughts and feelings warred within him, knowing what was supposed to happen this day.

"Being given to each other in our own lives, well, we owe just about anything we can give," he said up at the cowboy. Gavin surely understood that statement.

"And so, my wife, who you would call a doctor of science in this day and age, whipped up these bullets for you from metallicized hydrogen. And they will do the trick of killing those things out there better than your own bullets ever will.

"Kill as many of them as you and your friends can, Gavin Malloy. Every one of them dead will bring us closer to winning this thing one day."

With that, the middle-aged man slowly faded from sight, leaving behind a comfortable feeling that Gavin would meet him again someday.

Gavin turned and looked at his brother Colt, and the rest of the men, the Don included, and nodded his head at the box of bullets sitting serenely in the sand under the bridge of stone high overhead.

They could use all the help they could get, Gavin thought to himself, as Colt handed him up a cold handful of deadly ammo for his guns.

He prayed a silent prayer that they'd receive all that help, just as the Father promised him the day before.

It still wouldn't change anything, Gavin thought as he loaded the new silvery bullets into his six shooters. But it might assure that his brother and the men and women he cared about would live through this day, and many more to come.

That's all that mattered to Gavin as the silence of the moment was broken by an ear-rending scream from some freak of dark wings and sharp things standing at the tail end of the canyon before them.

While everyone around him flinched and cowered at the sound, Gavin took aim at the dark thing as it ran toward his people, and he took it out, a silver bullet hitting it right between the eyes and extinguishing the dark green light behind them.

Chapter 37

There were three unexpected miracles performed that dark, fateful day. All of which, more than likely, saved every human in the vicinity of the disastrous and thundering battle fought for the survival of all existence.

The first, and most practical, was that the magical box of bullets made from the shining metal given by the man named Benjamin never ran out. It overflowed with ammo, no matter how many handfuls of shiny bullets were removed.

The second was the surprising appearance of not one, but two separate armies to help the cowboys, two ladies, and legions of angels fight the overwhelming darkness spewing from the broken crags of the top of the high mountain to the West.

And the third and deciding miracle of the whole damn thing, was that Gavin did not, in fact, die that day. Or for many days afterward.

But his whole life was surely changed. In every way imaginable.

So, as the strange man with the strange accent faded from view, and Gavin Malloy took the first shot of the entire battle for the men and women atop horseback, Gavin's mind was on his impending doom.

As a group they moved out onto the valley floor, to vanquish as many of the dark things as they could, and Gavin, having no notion he would survive this day, fought like there was no tomorrow.

From out of the deep crevice in the ground, the glowing land bridge finally dull and normal behind them, rode a posse of cowboys and two women, guns blazing, horse hooves kicking up a literal storm of snow and mud, and the darkness fell before them.

Gavin Malloy rode point, directing his men and two women to the hottest part of the battle on the deep valley floor. Dark dog-like creatures rose up before the saddle-mounted cowboys, and each fell from a silver bullet made from the magical metal.

Larger things, with spread wings as dark as the ArchAngels were bright, ran alongside or flew overhead at the small group of dusty, worn cowpokes. And they, too, fell to the roaring of iron-packed steel.

Gavin looked out of the corner of his eye at his brother, Colt, who rode beside him, reins wrapped around his saddle horn, Winchester rifle spewing death before him. A pride rose up in Gavin's chest, and mixed with the heady feeling of invincibility, screamed into the onslaught of terrible things before them.

The thundering hooves of fourteen horses, spread in a straight line, made the sounds around them fade a bit in Gavin's ears, but not before the air-splitting roar of cannon fire filled his senses.

It came from off to his right, atop a ridge stationed at the eastern end of the large valley floor.

What met Gavin's eyes when he looked up on top of that ridge was unbelievable. He felt he was back at Appomattox. Or even more so, atop the ridge at Gettysburg.

The images transposed themselves in his mind and before his eyes as he spied a Union army, itself striking at the heart of the dark mass gathering on the valley floor and in the skies above it.

He wondered long enough at what he was seeing that he dropped his six shooters to his thighs, and almost caught his own death when arrows whizzed by his ears, shrieking in the cold winter winds.

Gavin yelled over the booming cannons and the ear-splitting fighting going on over their heads at Rye Harrison riding her mare next to him.

"Stay behind me, girl!"

He saw her look his way and nod. She pulled reins and her horse fell in lockstep behind Mabel.

He aimed his horse toward the right, seeing familiarity in the Union Army, and uncertainness everywhere else. When in the midst of battle, you sought out allies and someone to watch your back. It was lesson number one.

The men around him turned with him, and galloped up the shorter, shallow side of the mesa ridge that the army sat atop of. As he pulled Mabel short of the leading left flank line of the soldiers, an even louder voice shook him, and he couldn't quite understand why.

"Daddy!" Rye Harrison screamed, almost in his ear.

And as Gavin and Colt Malloy both saw the grey-haired man sitting up on his pure white horse, behind the lines of soldiers and canons, Gavin's stomach dropped worse than any other time since they set out from home, middle of last year.

He didn't know why, but he was more afraid of the general sitting, giving orders and pointing to weak spots in the enemy lines below. Now that they had rescued his daughter, there was no way to know if he would go back on his word to pardon the two Malloy's.

Looking quickly over at his big brother, he saw the concern and confusion on Colt's face, doubling the feelings of dread that swept over him suddenly.

The general heard his daughter's scream, turned toward the men riding up on top to join with the soldiers, and kicked his own horse hard in the flanks.

"Well, here we go," Gavin said under his breath, holstering his guns, squaring his shoulders, and getting ready for the hangman's noose.

Chapter 38

The reunion was swift but soft. The old man's face at first tightened up, but then relaxed, and the smile amidst the death and ruin around them all was a balm to their exposed nerves.

But not for many. Certainly not for the Malloy brothers.

The general had dismounted with a dexterity that defied his age, and his only daughter sprang from her horse as well.

They met in the middle of cannon fire and rifle barrages aimed at a nightmare most couldn't comprehend.

Pulling his daughter into his finely-pressed dark blue uniform brought solace to him and her, but the men around them could barely take their eyes off of the enemy. Only the Malloy brothers and the general's ever-present aide-de-camp, Lt. General Walter Mondaulk, witnessed the reunion.

Pushing her away to arm's length, the general looked over his daughter, checking her up and down to make sure she wasn't harmed in any way.

And he knew not a hair on her head had been damaged. He was mighty glad for that. *Mighty glad*, he thought as he looked her over, his eyes beginning to shine with tears.

"Well, lass, you've made it home," was all he could say.

She could hear the tears in her father's voice. But, as always, he swallowed his humanity, and swung his eyes away from her, back to the men who had joined his army atop the bluff, and especially at the two men he had commissioned to find his daughter.

The Malloy brothers sat horseback, looking placidly back at the general, despite the sounds of warring still going on around them all.

The general's eyes narrowed suddenly, and looking at everyone the brothers had brought with them, focused on the other woman within their midst.

"I assume the people who were responsible for the abduction of my daughter have been brought to justice, or brought here to face it," he told Gavin Malloy.

Gavin didn't even turn his head. He knew what could happen here.

"They were, General. Every last one of them," he told the old man.

"Then show me their heads, Gavin Malloy. That was the deal we had," the general said.

The air around the group turned cold as no one made a move. Gavin could feel Stace Lynn Craves getting ready to march her horse forward, and he needed to make sure that didn't happen.

And so, he spoke up, possibly condemning himself and Colt forever. He figured this was the moment that Archer Wisdom had told him about the afternoon before.

"They've been taken care of, General, and you have your daughter back. I suggest we part ways, and let bygones be bygones."

As he knew would happen, the general's face turned red, he made a quick gesture to the lieutenant general sitting horseback behind him, and suddenly Gavin's whole group was surrounded by rifles pointed right at them.

And Gavin's men all had their own guns pointed right back at the soldiers around them, those that weren't otherwise occupied with the falling death and darkness spewing from the mountaintop leagues away still.

The tension could be cut with a knife.

It was stress incarnate, and a falling snowflake in the wrong eye in that precise moment could end the lives of many innocents.

No one breathed.

No one moved.

No one said a word.

The stillness grew more and more solid as the seconds ticked by.

Gavin Malloy took a deep breath, his pistols in both hands not moving a centimeter as they pointed right at the head of the general who had almost destroyed his and his brother's lives more times than he wanted to count.

And that's when Rye Harrison strolled into the middle of the group of gun-toting men, and put a hand on Gavin's leg, sitting rigidly in his left stirrup.

As their eyes locked, time stopped.

The snow falling loose and easy around them seemed to slow, and as Gavin watched Rye's bright blue eyes blink one time, and then two, slower than molasses on a winter morning, a screech filled the air.

Darkness fell amongst them, with black feathers and golden talons replacing the clean, crisp snow that had swirled lazily around them all.

General Harrison was picked up by something with razor blade-like talons and eyes dark with green light, and his scream was the precursor to blood exploding all around.

Gavin Malloy did the only thing he could think to do as death rained down around them. He grabbed Rye Harrison's hand where it still lay against his leg, pulled her bodily into the saddle in front of him, and yelled bloody murder at his brother and his men.

He would let the army do the dying, while he and his men found a better place to fight from.

The sudden death of the general was the first and last thing on his mind as they kicked their horses into high speed and ran for the back of the mesa top they were upon, seeking shelter and a chance to take a breath before the next big thing happened.

And as the horses raced towards groupings of bush and bracken, rocks strewn about like a game of tiddlywinks played by giants, a roar filled the air that made all of the noise previously made seem like whispers.

Gavin looked around wildly, expecting sharp, dark death to descend at any moment, and feeling damn lucky to be alive through everything that had happened so suddenly, and what he saw made the already cold sweat running down his back freeze in place, solid.

For what he saw emerge from the mountaintop leagues to the west damn near stopped his heart cold.

A giant demon, or angel, something so large it couldn't even be described, climbed from the mountain like the mountain was a simple bump in a gravel lane. The thing was on fire, and death and destruction rained from it like the harbinger of apocalypse it had to be.

The thing was so large, Gavin couldn't even see all of it. And he could feel the world start tipping toward it, almost shaking them from his horse. He felt like the way he was going on even ground was tipped upward, and they were trying to ride uphill suddenly.

Asherah, the wife of God, arose from the mountaintop, reducing it to mere rubble, and the world itself felt her weight and presence finally upon it, and physically shifted because of it.

Gavin breathed in as deep as he could, mustered his mental and physical strength, squared his shoulders and thought one final thought to himself before riding hellbent and screaming into the storm.

"Well, they don't call me 'Against All Odds' for nothing."

And thunder and death rode with him into battle, once again.

Chapter 39

Samuel Tennyson was, by all accounts, a crazy drunk.

But he had come from a long line of men who had been considered 'lucky,' and he was out to prove he had the family luck as well.

That meant, to him, the purchasing of a spot of land in 'no man's land' and prospector'n there for gold.

He would get gold out of this damn clay, he figured, or die trying. Even in the wintery cold winds, the fever for riches untold kept the skinny, bearded man working from sunup to sundown.

Now, old Samuel Tennyson was no man's fool, for sure. And he had a surefire way to assure he got the gold, and no bandit or scamper could steal it out from under him. He had a plan, and follow that plan, he did.

So he staked claim to an old Indian wasteland, set up his digs on the side of a very promising hill, a hill that just felt right to him, and as he started to dig into the side of the lucky hill, he also built himself a damn nice little home around the front side of his mine.

He figured from the outside, it'd look like he was just living peaceful-like, with naught but an old mule in the fenced yard outside the timber and mud home. But inside the dwelling, he was busy as a bee, burrowing into the soft clay of southern Utah Territory, and finding pebbles and sand of the deepest golden color.

He would strike it rich as rich, and as soon as he had a good size lot of the golden gravel, he'd hightail it east, selling the gold a tooth-size nugget at a time.

A wild, windy cold had blown down from the north that gray day, but Samuel Tennyson was deep in the warm darkness of his personal mine, and no one was the wiser.

That was, until the large hill around him started shaking and dirt drifted down onto his mangy straw hat enough to stop the fever that overtook him most days for the gold that was due him.

The shaking didn't stop, and he knew his mine wasn't exactly up to safety standards. He'd best get out if the earth was going to quake him right out of his boots. Better to start the digging all over again than to die in a grave he had dug himself.

So, he took off running back toward the bright light of day, and the fire he had left smoldering in the fireplace.

As Samuel Tennyson cleared out of the large hole taking up one whole wall of his living room, he could hear old

Betty, his mule, screaming out in the fenced-in pen he kept her in.

He ran outside with the world around him still shaking and shuddering, to grab old Betty and do the only thing he could think of. He took her back inside the cabin with him.

They were huddled in the far corner of his gray-washed timber home, waiting for the shaking and booming and carrying-on to give way, when Betty started braying and trying to get away from the hole in the side of the hill, what made up one whole wall of his home.

He saw a light within the mine that shouldn't have been there. And all Samuel Tennyson could do was wonder at what kind of devil he had unknowingly let loose from his digging into the Utah clay these many years.

The light grew brighter, the shaking grew worse, and as the mountain top off to the west of his north-facing home blew its top, like the largest volcano eruption ever recorded on God's green earth, with the light deep in his mine coming closer, Samuel Tennyson bent low in fear and cowered, wetting himself in terror of his encroaching death.

He heard voices from deep in his mine, and as his brain conjured up all kinds of devils and evils coming from deep within the earth, two people walked, happy as could be, out of the front hole and right into his living room.

"Well met, sir," the taller of the strange looking people said to Samuel. Sam could barely make out the man's accent, but his English was good enough, he reckoned. Samuel Tennyson stood up behind old Betty, holding to her harness so she wouldn't go screaming and braying, knocking all his handmade furniture to hell.

Samuel just stood behind Betty like she was a shield of some sort. The unfamiliar and feminine looking lady of the pair smiled at him, and he felt his heart melt right through his boots.

When she spoke, the heavens opened up, and sun shone down on old poor Samuel Tennyson.

"It's a beautiful home you have here, Sam," she said, with just the most darling lilt to her voice. She sounded like music to Samuel Tennyson's ears.

"Don't mind us barging through here, Sam," she said to calm him and ol' Betty down. The woman walked up to the pair of them and stroked Betty's neck. Sam wished she'd touch him too.

"We are going to be using your mine as a way into this world, Sam, so you're going to see a lot of men and women come through here." He just nodded dumbly at her.

"They are going to all look like my husband there," she said. And that's when Sam looked back over at the man who had walked out of the earth with this angel standing before him. Sam finally noticed the man's tall, strong frame, and the striking eyes that peered back at him, seeing everything but looking like they didn't see anything at all.

The whites of the man's eyes covered his entire eyeballs, and Sam had only seen that one other time before, on a street preacher, blind as a bat, back down in New Orleans. The old, blind preacher had been asking for money. Begging almost. Samuel had dropped a few coins he couldn't really afford to part with, but the old beggar looked as if he needed them more.

The man now looking down on Samuel Tennyson there in his own home, taller than just about any man he had ever seen before, smiled suddenly, and Sam could see what the beautiful woman standing in front of him saw in the taller man.

"You can call me Facecake," the angel said to Sam. He turned his eyes back to the lovely woman.

"And this is my husband, Abraham," she said. Sam could still only nod along. The whole ordeal seemed a dream.

"We are going to march an army right through your living room here, Sam, but I promise, nothing will be broken, and we will make sure you have all the gold ol' Betty here can carry when we're through, okay?" she asked him. He nodded at the angel stupidly again. *What kind of name for an angel was 'Facecake'?* he asked himself as Betty calmed under her petting.

"Alright Sam, we have to get out there to the fighting before it turns the wrong way," she said.

And with that, a whole horde of dark-haired, taller-than-should-be humans carrying strange metal cylinders ran from out of his mine, through his home, and out the doors into the falling cold, and shaking world.

As the men and women, white-eyes all of them, ran through his home, the tallest of them, the angel's husband, walked up to him, and looked down on poor old Sam Tennyson. The man's face lit up in the biggest grin once again, and he put out a hand twice as large as Sam's.

Sam took Abraham's hand and couldn't help but smile back up at the man and his pure white eyes.

"I've always wanted to see the Old West," the man said to Sam. Sam still had no idea what any of them were talking about, but he could just start to hear an even bigger commotion happening outside.

He turned his eyes back to the tall man gripping his hand in his own.

"Yes, sir, the Wild West. 1870. Right after the Civil War. What an honor it is to be here, Sam. An honor indeed," he said.

Sam just smiled through his whiskers back up at the tall man.

As the too-tall man joined his wife and two other men who looked remarkably like him, Sam remembered his manners, and shouted after the four people leaving his home. It grew suddenly cold in their absence.

"I'll put the coffee on, then," he screamed into the tempest taking place what seemed right outside his home.

He couldn't get the image of the remarkably beautiful woman who had called herself Facecake, or the too-tall man named Abraham, out of his mind, even after his entire world exploded.

A nightmare crashed into the world, from out of the mountains to his west, and he would never be the same again.

He watched as the white-eyed army clashed with something so dark and terrible, and a familiar Union army clashed with shiny Beings he couldn't even comprehend.

All he could think to do was start crawling back into his mine and covering his head and ears. It was the only sensible thing old Samuel Tennyson could think of. His mind shattered, and his wits scattered as he watched a devil the size of mountains and seas escape into the vast valley and hollow world right outside his little home, and wreak holy hell unto the mountains all around.

And that's how they would find old Samuel Tennyson after it was all said and done. Curled up deep within his mine, old Betty holding vigil for the corpse caught up against a vein of gold so bright and rich, it shone with its own light.

But the scream frozen on old dead Samuel Tennyson's face told the tale that he hadn't even seen he had struck it richer then rich.

No man should have been witness to the horrors and hell that day brought to the world outside the old poor man's doorstep.

Facecake looked up at her husband Abraham, who was looking down on the old poor man.

"Guess his luck held out in the end anyway," she said. Abraham nodded.

"Yeah," he told his beautiful and long-suffering wife. "No one should be living here, with what's about to happen."

And with that, the pair, along with their white-eyed army, disappeared back into the earth, where Abraham was most comfortable, but which Facecake knew was just the doorway to their home in Heaven. And had been, for thousands and thousands of years.

Chapter 40

Guns firing to the left and the right, and his reins tied around Mabel's saddle horn, Gavin Malloy sat saddle, killing anything that moved in front of him. He could hear his brother, Colt, and their men along with them – *the Don's men*, he corrected in his mind – behind him doing the same.

But the numbers of the dark beasts and deadly things flying overhead were overwhelming. Any second and he knew they would be overrun, despite the masses of bright, shiny heavenly Beings fighting alongside him and his men.

He didn't want to look up and see the monstrosity walking toward the battle. With every one of her footsteps, everything around Gavin seemed to jump and then to settle back down. He could do nothing except allow his instincts and fast reactions to keep him alive as long as he could. He felt death looming every second of the battle.

What was seeming like hours were mere minutes. In the heat of the battle and fighting, with darkness descending down on him and his men, everything slowed down to a crawl, but his mind worked faster than it had ever done before.

He had time to look up for just a second, and see the ArchAngel Host in the air sing victoriously as something just as large as the demon stalking the battle appeared atop a mesa the size of the state of Montana to the south.

The rejoining of those two towering Beings made what was happening on the earth seem like a Sunday stroll in the park.

The tall Being, in shiny armor like that the ArchAngels wore, grabbed ahold of the fiery demon, and they both rose into the air. A heat shimmer that Gavin could not explain seemed to ripple out from the bottom of the two behemoths, and Gavin couldn't quite understand how he knew, but he knew that the taller of the two had forced them both into another Plane of existence.

One that was finally seen in the Material Plane, where it had never been seen before.

The skies above the battle turned as dark as night, and the stars shone down bright enough to touch. The darkness of the sky of the Spiritual Plane made the battlefield treacherous and deep, and Gavin could barely keep ahold of Mabel as the dark demons and dog-like creatures found new fervor.

And that was when the darkness around Gavin lit up in brightest hues of rainbow colors. He had never seen anything like it. But it didn't originate from the skies above him, displaying the Heavens of the Spiritual Plane.

These colors that lit up the Utah desert around him, and made the falling snow shine like the brightest campfire, came from tubes being carried by a human army that had appeared out of nowhere.

The lights were surely pretty, he thought, but when the beams of light hit the darkness of the enemy hellbent on killing them all, the darkness burst apart in sprays of greenest ochre and bright blood.

The too-tall humans, which Gavin could barely make out as Mabel reared up against another tide of darkness, burned down the enemy like scything grass with the cylinders they carried.

Each cylinder emitted the bright lights, and the darkness died as a result. Gavin still couldn't wrap his mind around what he was seeing. He pulled reins near the bottom of a mesa, to catch his breath, reload, and find his bearings. He not only felt and heard, but could now see his men, and by some sheer luck, the two women who had accompanied them this far, pull up reins next to him.

He saw tears in the eyes of Rye Harrison, but in the midst of the deepening darkness and booming fighting going on around them all, he didn't have time to comfort the woman after the brutal death of her own father.

He also saw many of the Union soldiers, those who had been on horseback, follow him and his men to the base of the mesa as well. He guessed with the sudden lack of leadership, those who could follow him had done just that.

So, looking around at the small army he himself had gathered, he took stock of what he could. The men passed around the metallic and seemingly magical bullets to the soldiers, and when everyone was breathing regularly again, Gavin nodded toward Colt and the Don, and pulled the highest-ranking soldier from amongst the cavalry to him. He saw it was a youngish lieutenant, and therefore he felt right in passing down orders, as Gavin himself had achieved the rank of captain during the Civil War.

The battles and wars he had fought during that bloody time held not even a candle breath to what he was witnessing this day.

Looking up at the firmament above them, the entirety of the heavens opened up for all to see, Gavin wondered at just what the hell he was doing here.

And then looking down at Rye Harrison, who was wiping her nose on a handkerchief she had managed to procure from somewhere, and then at the stricken and confused faces of the men looking back at him for leadership, he figured he was right where he was supposed to be.

Finally, remembering the words of Archer Wisdom from the day before, he knew deep in his heart that his being there at that battle, and Colt as well, gave them both Absolution and Redemption from the past they had shared and the atrocities they had committed.

He and his brother, the infamous and feared Malloy brothers, were finally free of their debt of sins, and they could live their lives, if they made it through this battle, knowing they had earned forgiveness from on High.

With that final thought in his mind, and seeing the clarity and understanding in his big brother's eyes as well, Gavin's breath came deep and clean, and he found new resolve for what he had to do.

Finally speaking for the first time since he had sat back on the mesa top right before General Harrison had been pulled into the sky and to his death, he told those around him exactly what they wanted to hear.

"We are going to push for the middle. Join back-to-back with those tall people out there all alone, and let's finish this damn thing… while whatever is going on up there in the sky decides what happens this day," he said.

Many heads nodded around him, looking up into the deep space and bright stars above them, where the two giants fought in slow motion, and he heard the pure ringing sound of hammers being pulled back, and rifles being cocked.

As a unit, the men, women, and soldiers around Gavin Malloy took deep breaths, tightened reins and saddle girths, and aimed a hundred magical, silvery bullets at an enemy they still couldn't understand.

But to a man they followed Gavin Malloy into the thickest and hottest of the fighting, and even as some fell to sword, arrow, and hooked talons, many more made it to the center, to meet up with the army of white-eyed men and women.

And pressing back-to-back, they fought off the demon horde, against all odds, and as successfully as they could, only being human, of course.

The men and women that day fought like demons themselves, and they had to. The very existence around them demanded that they do so, as the alternative was too much to comprehend.

And only being human, the ArchAngels who looked down on the mass of fighting and movement on the plains of no-man's land thought to themselves, *was enough to win this day, and this battle.*

Raguel himself, clad in deepest blue armor, as it moved and morphed around him, took a second from the fighting, looked down on the Malloy brothers and saw what the Father had told him so long ago.

Those two would rise to the occasion as the Father needed them to, with only a gentle push, and the forgiveness and redemption they had both sought with all of their hearts.

The pride and awe the ArchAngel Raguel had for those two men kept him fighting the Watcher horde, even as his brothers and sisters within the Host gave ground to an enemy they were finally understanding, after all.

Inter-Mission 2

The Firmament broke, the Planes of Existence collided together, and with the weight of the other existences pressing on both, a *snap* was heard throughout the galaxies and in all three Planes.

The Creator of All didn't know why His Will didn't stop the encroaching darkness. He didn't know why He couldn't just vanquish the fiery Devil of Asherah from His Creation.

He didn't even know where She came from, or how She existed in the first place.

He had not known a lot of things over the last few centuries, but what He did know was that nothing was as it should be.

As He swung his mighty Sword at the Demon's head, She blocked it with Her black talons, and with a mighty scream that shook the Heavens, She cut back at the Creator with all She had.

His only advantage was that Asherah had come to His Creation, where She did not hold sway. That advantage in the Spiritual and Material Realms was all that kept it all from falling to utter darkness, like it had been when He Spoke, and the Darkness had been pushed back, at the beginning of Time.

The Demon Asherah sliced at the Creator's face once again, but He held Her back with but a wave of His hand. Stepping back, the Creator saw the opening He needed, and with that opening, He Willed His Sword into the creature's very middle. A scream like a million hurricanes shook the Heavens, the Firmament, and the Battleground below them.

Wounded, and in utter shock, the Demon and Her horde disappeared from His Creation like they had never been there at all. Looking down at the Battlefield, even the dead of the Darkness disappeared, but their destruction remained.

He called his Host home, and watched as the humans below took stock of the day-long battle, and their own deaths.

He was beyond proud of His humans, and that His plan had been a success. He knew, as did the Host, that the humans were needed in ways they couldn't quite figure yet. But with the help of the humans this day, the Creator was able to vanquish the demon horde and their Mother back to the existence from whence they had come.

As His Host appeared in the Heavens around Him, and the Firmament solidified, blocking the Planes from each other, He took stock Himself of what had happened, and what would be needed going forward.

He knew, and saw the same knowledge in the looks He saw on the faces of His ArchAngel Host, that this battle was only the beginning, and until the Creator Himself got to the very bottom of all that was happening, the Battles would continue to grow, and increase in both intensity and frequency.

But that was for another day. As for this day, His Son Raguel came to the Throne and bowed low. The Creator knew what Raguel would ask.

So He answered His Son before the question could sound throughout the Throne Room.

"Yes my Son, I will give Gavin and Colt Malloy the rest they deserve."

The ArchAngel Raguel smiled up at his Father. But he, as well as the gathering Host also knew more truth than that.

And so, the Creator spoke to the doubts and questions in all of their eyes.

"But they will be needed again soon, my Son. Them, and all of the humans who have suffered the Missions I have set before them," the Creator spoke Doom to the Throne Room.

"For our enemy is but wounded and scared," He said. "They will return, or we will take the Battle to them."

With those words, the ArchAngel Host, and all of the Heavens, raised their voices and clashed their bladed weapons together in harmony. Too much had been lost for too long, and the Heavens, as well as those Below, were ready to exact Heavenly retribution upon their enemy's numbers.

The Creator was alone in His feelings of fear and trepidation. For He alone knew what it would take to finally vanquish this Foe.

And He would take this cup from His own lips if He could. But like the very Laws of His Nature, He could easier destroy everything than to go against what He knew would come.

Death begets Life. And everything had an Opposite.

They were His Laws, but they weren't. And the distinction between the two gave Him pause, as well as confusion.

He could stomach not knowing something. But to be confused by the very Nature He had set into motion… *Well, the Creator of Heavens and Earth thought to Himself, that was a whole 'nother level of wrongness in His Creation, and in all of The Other Creations that He had only just that moment become aware of.*

Chapter 41

Gavin dismounted from the saddle atop Mabel for the first time in what seemed like ages. His legs and buttocks screamed in pain at the change in place, but as he stomped his feet a few times on the hard, frozen gravel under his boots, the pain subsided, and the pins and needles gave way.

He had holstered his six shooters before dismounting, but he pushed them in until they set against the bottoms snuggly.

He certainly didn't need a pistol falling out of his holster as he met the tall humans who had almost single-handedly saved the day.

The Heavenly Armies were gone in a blink of an eye, and not a single scrap of evidence remained of the enemy who had taken so many lives. To have seen the absolute disappearance of both sets of Beings was unsettling.

Like a harsh and vindicative tornado that just up and swooshed back into the dark clouds from which it had come, taking all noise and death with it.

The leftover silence and settling of the earth around them made many ears pop and eyes go wide with the surprise of it.

Gavin knew that the Creator had been victorious in the Spiritual Realms above them, and even that thin layer of shimmering heat between the two Planes disappeared, bringing brightest day back into painful existence.

Walking toward the white-eyes that remained, all still holding the red-hot, smoking cylinders they had brought with them, and which had emitted such destruction amongst their enemies, Gavin looked around and tried to ascertain just what to do next.

He sauntered up to the tall man who seemed to be in charge. Introducing himself to the white-eyed man, he got the distinct feeling the man knew everything about Gavin, and things that Gavin didn't even know.

"I'm Gavin Malloy. We sure thank y'all for showing up like you did. We were getting pretty overran before y'all got here," he told the man. The tall man smiled down at Gavin.

"Well met, Gavin Malloy. Well met," he said.

The man stuck out his large hand, which Gavin took instantly.

"I'm Abraham Simone. My friends just call me Abe," he told Gavin.

For his sake, Gavin liked the man immediately. *He gave off a soothing feeling*, Gavin thought as a tall, beautiful woman walked up to the pair of them, their hands still shaking between them.

"This is my wife, her name is Alexandria, but everyone calls her 'Facecake,'" the taller man said.

Gavin nodded to the woman, pulling the brim of his straw hat down with the nod. She smiled at the cowboy, but noticing something behind Gavin, smiled even wider over his shoulder.

Gavin turned and saw Rye Harrison walking up to the group. The rest of his men had unhorsed, and walked among the white-eyed men and women, giving salutations and shaking hands.

The foursome of Gavin, Rye, Facecake, and Abe stood looking at each other in easy silence, the two taller members smiling down at the two shorter. Gavin and Rye, if they was honest with themselves, felt that the other couple knew so much more than what was currently happening around them.

Abe broke the silence first.

"Gavin Malloy, I've been told to tell you that when this battle was over, you've earned your rest, and your Redemption," he told Gavin.

Gavin wasn't quite sure what to make of that, as questions upon questions reverberated around in his mind. But as he felt Rye Harrison take his hand, and Facecake smile at them both, it dawned on him that asking questions would just be a waste of time. He sure wasn't going to look a gift horse in the mouth.

Rye squeezed Gavin's hand tightly and then let go. She and the woman, Facecake, walked off a bit to speak quietly together. The two men watched the women as they put their heads together, telling secrets nether men would understand, most like.

Abe slapped Gavin on the shoulder harder than he meant to, but Gavin took it quietly. When he looked up at the taller man, a wisdom and knowing shone out of his white eyes. Gavin didn't know how he knew what he felt, but it just seemed right.

"Gavin, I'm going to tell you something of the future. It shouldn't hurt anything, and you've a right to know a few things," Abe told him. Gavin just braced himself for more revelations. He wondered just how much his already fragile mind could take with what all had happened that day.

"Facecake and I are from the future. Way in the future, and not on this planet either," the man told Gavin. Gavin just listened, absorbing the words, and knew he would ponder over them all for years to come.

"We both died, and as we died, we were taken to what you call Heaven," Abe said.

"When we got there, and reunited, we were told by the same ArchAngels that had watched over our lives and the lives of all of our loved ones that we were meant for even more than what we had done while alive," he said.

"It was then that we saw the extent of the enemy's encroachment on this Creation, and were put to work fighting the enemy, which we had done for most of our actual lives," Abe told the cowboy.

"A fight that's still ongoing, as you could see today, and a fight that I'm afraid you and your men will join once your own lives are over," Abe said.

"You're given the rest of your natural lives, Gavin, to rest, and enjoy as much of this world as you can. And you should. You should come to love this world and this Plane as much as you can, because doing so will keep you in the fight once it's your turn," Abe finished.

"And when it is your turn, Gavin, you and your brother will be conscripted into a much larger war than the War of the States that you were forced into.

"But when that time comes, we will be there to welcome you as brothers and sisters, and finish this thing for all time," Abe said.

"That's been promised. We just have no idea what that's going to look like. But we know you and Colt will be a big part of it, just like we are ourselves," he finally said.

Gavin just nodded. The ArchAngel Raguel had told him something of the same. And as the pieces fell into place for Gavin Malloy, he wondered if even he knew more than this tall man was telling him.

He didn't have long to ponder that feeling, as the two women rejoined them.

It was getting late in the day, and Gavin knew that he and his men needed to find shelter and take stock of what supplies they had left, and what was to be done with the separate groups that had come together to fight a common enemy.

The two pairs set off in different directions after long goodbyes had been said. It seemed much too soon, but also too long for Gavin as he and Rye, hand in hand, walked back toward the picket lines of horses and their men.

Colt and Stace Lynn joined him and Rye, and got set to figuring things out as the white-eyed army, led by the husband and wife team of Abraham and Alexandria Simone, disappeared back to where they came from.

As he lay his head down that night, right next to the already sleeping, and mourning, Rye Harrison, he said the first prayer of his life to a Creator he had known as a friend and mentor. He looked forward to a bit of rest, but knew that bigger, harder, and much more frightening things were ahead for them all.

His prayers mixed that night with many more said around the two campfires laid out for the sleeping cowboys and two women. Not a soul amongst them could believe what all they had seen that day, and as the night unfolded, and peace lay about the land around, they all felt the comforting hand of their Savior, giving peace and rest where only upheaval and pain had existed earlier.

Chapter 42

The first task of the new morning was to find, bury, and memorialize their dead. The first body that Gavin and Colt came across made the rest of the day agonizing at best.

Their old friend, Don Celso Baca, had taken an arrow to the heart in the heat of the worst of the fighting the day before. In all of the easy distractions after the battle, the brothers had not noticed the older man's absence.

Colt and Gavin happened upon the Don's body before his two sons did, and so lightened the blow to the boys in advance. But the two sons of the Don, both Dons themselves now, were easy acquaintances with Death, and only shed tears in private, upon returning their father's body to his beloved home in Santa Rosa, a week later.

Gavin and Colt Malloy, however, mourned their old friend for seasons to come, even taking a long put-off trip back down to New Mexico Territory, years later, to advocate for the Territory to become a State of the United States. That feat wouldn't happen until the early winter of 1912.

The brothers, meanwhile, mourned their old friend, and visited his grave on that future trip to apologize for taking the old man into the greatest battle the world had ever seen. The Don's family, predictably, still loved the two men, and poured blessings and thanksgiving on the brothers when they visited.

Standing alone the day after the battle, not knowing the future, or what would become of the Don's favored Santa Rosa, the brothers felt unabashedly guilty for taking the old man on his last trail ride.

The death of the great man wasn't the only blow to come that day. It was merely the first.

Many of the soldiers that had ridden with General Harrison, including the old general himself, had perished in the fighting.

When the call went up that scouts from the military unit had found the general's body, Gavin did all he could to keep Rye from seeing her father torn apart by the darkness that had almost consumed them all. She listened to Gavin's report on the death of her father with a stoic face, but he knew she would want all the details.

And so, without her having to see the gruesome scene herself, he described it in enough detail for her later that night, so she was able to put to rest her initial anger, and then resentment, at her father, and at the Army who had taken him.

The old man's body had been strewn about atop the mesa they had perched upon at the beginning of the fighting. He had been torn limb from limb, and except for his uniform identifying who he was, there would have been no way to know. The general's head was never found, and the rest of him looked gnawed upon. As if giant vultures had taken large bites out of the old man's hide.

His aide-de-camp, Light General Walter Mondaulk took command of what soldiers were left to the unit that had been sent to hunt enemy Indian scouts, and headed back east. Not another word was heard from the man, nor the Army, in all of the Malloy brothers' lives.

They assumed, over the next few years, that they had received their pardons, if ever the Army had wanted them in the first place. After the confusion of the Civil War had disbanded, many such men like the Malloy's were given grace and not sought after. The United States would be long in mending the bloody war, but where the Malloy's were concerned, they were left to their own devices, and freedoms, thereafter.

After the Union soldiers marched off, without so much as a 'by-your-leave,' the Don's men, now under the command of his oldest son, Shooter, took off south as well.

That parting had taken a lot longer than the one with the Army, and many tears were shed for what could have been, or what should have been. The Malloy brothers watched their oldest friend's sons take his wrapped body back south, to be buried in the place he had loved the most.

The man who had accompanied them since they had left Montana Territory that summer also went with the Don's men. The Irishman, Russ O'Shanashay, the man who had loved their friend Heath, rode south with the Don's men, and the brothers never heard another word about him, to their chagrin. You couldn't ride trail with a man for so long, and not feel anything for him, or his future, Gavin said more than once.

And finally, that just left Gavin and Colt Malloy, with Rye Harrison and Stace Lynn Craves, trying to figure out just what the hell they were all going to do now. It took several days to figure that out, and several more to enact the plan the four had come up with.

Three months after the horrific battle in southern Utah Territory, and almost exactly nine months to the day after the brothers had set off from their ranch at the foot of Old Bald Top, Montana Territory, they drove a large, covered wagon, with a line of horses extending behind, through the gates of their home.

The young man, Porter, was the first to see the brothers through the afternoon mists of the late spring day and, whooping and hollering, he ran all the way from the front of the ranch house to the gates, to see what the brothers had brought home this time.

And smiling a smile bigger than the Montana sky overhead, he saw that the brothers had each brought home a wife, and Porter knew nothing would ever be the same again.

Chapter 43

Years and years and adventures and adventures later, Gavin Malloy sat atop a different mare than his old horse Mabel. That old mare had lived longer than anyone had figured possible, but even the most perfect of horses, reared in battle, and having a personality almost human-like, had to succumb to Nature.

And that's just what the old girl had done, two years after the brothers had brought their new brides home from the West Coast, where they had married the two women in San Fransisco.

Gavin, atop the tall ridge running high to the north of his lands, looked down once again at the patchworks that made up the Malloy Ranch. It was Nineteen and Sixteen, and Gavin Malloy was eighty-one years old.

The years since the Great Battle in Utah had been kind to the old man, but like Mabel, everything eventually succumbs to Nature. His deeply lined face and sore muscles attested to that fact. As did the knowledge and wisdom that only comes with old age lived correctly.

The ranch below was bustling in the late summer sunshine. More than forty workers tilled away at the farmland he had acquired sometime around the turn of the century.

More hands worked the horses being trained and raised to work the cattle that took up a third more of the land he had purchased using funds his wife had inherited from her own late father.

Gavin had secretly felt the general owed he and his brother much more than that, and wasn't at all ashamed of using the money Rye had inherited to make them all the more successful.

Gavin's old eyes looked down on the twin homes he and his brother had built to either end of their new lands the summer after they had returned from the west. Colt and Stace had produced four strapping sons and one daughter, sweet as their mother had turned. Old Snakebite McGee had died in the Great Battle, and Stace Lynn Malloy had arisen from the ashes to make his brother an honest, and teetotaling man through the next forty-six years.

Every member of the Colt Malloy family had purchased, fought for, worked, and enlarged the land about to make the Malloy Ranch the biggest in all the state of Montana.

Gavin and his beautiful wife, the daughter of the general, Rye Malloy, had added a pair of sons to the mess. Both boys were raised now, and had families of their own.

And unlike the scions of Colt Malloy, Gavin and Rye's sons had moved down south, finding adventures of their own. They still wrote and sent telegrams early every month, but Gavin didn't expect those two boys to get into any less trouble than their father and uncle before them.

And so Gavin was content as could be. He looked down on a whole valley teeming with activity and profits that he and his brother had built with their two hands, and more bullets than he cared to think of.

The horse under him whinnied, scooting nearer the stallion Rye rode next to Gavin. He smiled over at his wife of more than forty-five years. She was still as beautiful and still as the morning dew under their horse's shod hooves.

She smiled back at the only man she had ever loved, and looked up at the sky as Gavin looked down at the valley below.

And that had been the way of it, for over forty tranquil and loving years. Rye always had one eye on her husband, and one eye on the sky, as Gavin had his hands and attention deep in the dirt he had suffered and worked so hard for.

"Sky's getting darker, my love," Rye told her aging husband. She was still in the healthful vigor of late mid-life, and her older husband needed every hand he could get to keep moving through this life, making much more of a difference through his words and wisdom now than he ever did with pistols and man-hunting.

He nodded at his beautiful and dutiful wife, and nickered at the mare under him. Together, he and Rye rode back down the deep trail they had made together, riding to this very spot most days, as weather allowed, to look down on the legacy they were building together.

Late that night, as the cold of the mountain winds sang down into the valley, and the fire leaped high in the gratings to meet it, Gavin sat in his father's old chair, warming his bones, and looking down the long years of a life he was satisfied with.

His darling Rye had retired to their bed hours earlier, and he knew she would sleep like a rock. He loved that most about the younger woman. She had made his and Colt's lives so much better and richer, along with Stace Lynn, he couldn't give enough love and adoration back to the woman. But he knew in his heart that she had been happiest here in the valley.

Gavin Malloy stared deep into the fire, and knew what no one else on the ranch knew in that moment. As everyone all around the valley slept peacefully, and dreams of comfort and happiness settled into more beds and rooms than he could imagine, Gavin knew that tonight would be his last on this mortal plane.

And as if in answer to his thoughts, he heard a rustling behind him and smiled. It had been many years since he had been in the presence of Archer Wisdom, but there was no denying the glorious presence behind his chair. One never quite forgot meeting their Maker.

His thoughts making him smile, and knowing that they made Archer smile, was all the reward that Gavin Malloy needed. He was ready.

His thoughts briefly went to his wife, his brother, his sister-in-law, and his sons. But he had peace in his heart.

He knew better than most that death was merely a stepping into a new room, and not an ending at all. He had prepared his family and friends as much as was needed. They were all aware of the stories and history passed down over so many campfire tales and comfortable re-telling's of accounts from the past.

Gavin rose slowly to his feet. He stood strong, but it was a struggle at his age. He turned to Archer Wisdom, who leaned against the large wooden beam leading into the kitchen. A smile creased the old face, which hadn't aged a bit in the intervening years.

Gavin smiled back at the Creator in human guise, and nodded his head. He was ready to begin the fight. The fight that Abe Simone had warned him about, so many years ago.

Archer walked toward the old man standing before the fire, and said the last words that Gavin Malloy ever heard on the Material Plane. And after, the ArchAngel Raguel, hidden from Gavin behind the thick wooden beams of the log home, laid the soulless body of one of his favorite children back gently into the chair Gavin had risen out of to meet his Maker.

After receiving redemption and salvation so many years earlier, Gavin Malloy had earned the rest that he had taken, and all of the love, legacy, and history that he had left behind him.

Gavin nodded again at the Creator, standing as straight as he had in all the years in between. His heart raced at the thought of joining the trail once again, and fighting for all he was worth.

Smiling, Archer Wisdom stretched out his hand, and took Gavin's in his own, leading him away from his earthly home.

As bright light shone down on the pair, and heavenly music lifted for the first time to the ears of the man who had fought for half of his life, and then rested the other half, he smiled bright at the future in front of him.

"It's time, Gavin Malloy. It's time to take the fight to them."

The ArchAngel Raguel looked down on the body of Gavin Malloy one last time and smiled brighter. He was glad this particular Mission had come to a satisfying conclusion.

But his smile faltered a bit as he disappeared from the Material only to reappear in the Spiritual, to the loud ringing of blade against blade, and the screams of the dying.

This particular Mission was complete. But the fight had only just begun.

The End

Joshua Loyd Fox
Dec. 2022 – Nov. 2023

Epilogue

The Creator of All walked to the edge of a precipice, and looked down on a world they had only just left.

The ArchAngel Raphael, His very favored Son of Healing and Truth, walked up behind Him. They watched the nearly destroyed earth below. Nodding to Himself, the Creator looked over at the Light shining forth from His Son, and asked the question to the ArchAngel of the Elder Ilk that they had all wondered.

"How did the enemy encroach fully upon the earth to enact full Battle, my Son?" Raphael looked up at his Father and, un-angel-like, shrugged his confusion. The entire Host had debated it ad nauseum.

"I believe I know," the Creator told Raphael.

The Father took Raphael by the shoulder, which wasn't an uncomfortable or even scary movement. At one time, even coming close to the Creator's bodily countenance would bring instant death to the Ilk. The Father's Glory couldn't even be seen by mortals, lest their corporeal bodies exploded in easiest of flames.

But ever since the Dark Arrow had taken one of their own, the Father's Glory had left Him.

The pair suddenly winked out of existence in the Spiritual, and re-appeared in the Material, in a room that was familiar, although he couldn't place it, to Raphael.

It was a dark library room, with the brightest of sunshine out the tall windows. The landscape outside the windows suggested western Europe, but the ArchAngel couldn't place where he was, at first.

Until he felt but didn't see the sizzling of the rip in time and space that had recently been in place in the very corner of the room.

"Ahh," was all ArchAngel Raphael said to himself. The Creator merely nodded.

Below, both Beings could feel the Will being enacted by the children of the FateMaker. With that knowledge, Raphael suddenly knew right where they had apparated to in the Material.

The place where the Fate Maker, Kreo Fairchild, had disappeared into the Rift, following a Watcher, to speak to the very Wife of God, Asherah Herself.

"I fear," the Creator told His Son, "that our FateMaker may be being used against us."

Raphael almost didn't have the heart to say it, but knew that it needed to be said, nonetheless.

"Or he is in junction with the enemy, spiteful for the life we put him through," he told his Father.

The Creator merely nodded, seeing the children a few floors below them, and knowing that both children could feel their presences in turn.

"I'd rather err on the side of Right," the Creator said. "I'd rather face a truth of Kreo Fairchild being used against his wishes than for him to have turned against us." Raphael just shook his head. He didn't share in his Father's optimism.

"Either way, my Son, we cannot tread upon that existence without losing our very existence, so therefore, a mortal must follow the FateMaker, and ascertain his circumstances," the Creator told the ArchAngel.

They both looked down through the intervening floors, seeing the Will of both of the children of the FateMaker, and both knowing what would need to be done.

"There's no way, Father…" The ArchAngel Raphael said to his Father, the Maker of All.

The Creator cut him off with a look.

"It must be done, for all of *this* existence, my Son," the Creator said in admonishment.

The Creator faded from the Material, to gather His forces for another incursion. The ArchAngel Raphael looked forlornly through the floors to the children who used the gift of Will to play house.

"Goddamn it," Raphael mumbled under his breath, figuring out a way to get the two young humans to do what their own father could not do.

How he hated that this task had fallen to him. But he wouldn't be alone, he knew. No member of the Heavenly Host did any Mission alone anymore. And so, he sent out a Calling to his younger sister, Jophiel.

He would need Jophiel's beauty and kindness to sway the daughter of the FateMaker.

The ArchAngel Raphael looked back down at Emma and Charlie Fairchild and cursed under his breath again as his dark-pink-robed sister joined him in the library of the supposed turncoat, Kreo Fairchild.

Raphael's cussing didn't end any time soon as he and the ArchAngel Jophiel set to appearing before the Children of Willpower.

There was no way these two would be willing to enact the ultimate sacrifice, and at the same time, end the threat of their very own father, in the only way that would work.

They were to set child against parent.

And that had NEVER worked throughout all of human history.

"Goddamn it, indeed," Raphael thought out loud as the pair of ArchAngels disappeared from the dark library and reappeared amidst flying debris and loud rock music in the room below.

From the Author

Well, here we are again. With a laundry list of people to thank, and more motivation and personal challenges to follow dreams. With the conclusion of my sixth complete novel, and the fifth in this series in just under five years, it's no surprise that my life is nowhere near where it was when I started, and I can't even imagine where we are going to be in the next five years.

First and foremost, my thanks go out to my Heavenly Father, God, and His son, Jesus Christ. But I will get to that in the end of this. It just needed put first, as in everything I do.

I would like to begin by thanking my wife, the amazing author and editor, Heather Daughrity. This year has been a whirlwind of ups and downs, but no higher up than when you agreed to not only marry me, but to join in this crazy thing that we are both building and working toward.

Most of our fans know our story, but I'll briefly touch on it here.

Heather and I were Facebook friends for a couple of years before we tied the knot in a castle in the mountains of Colorado. A castle that shows up in this series multiple times. But back on Facebook, we were both a part of a growing family of indie authors and publishers. We were passing acquaintances, and had only met in real life a single time, when I invited her to my very first Barnes and Noble book signing early last year. She came, we met, we went our separate ways.

During the intermission, both our lives changed in drastic and parallel ways. Months later, when she reached out to invite me to an author event she was a big part of, we caught up with what we had both missed about the other's life. Putting two and two together, and realizing we were both in similar situations, and were mightily attracted to one another, we decided to throw caution to the wind (against the better judgment of just about everyone we knew) and see if we could use intentionality, resolve, compromise, and pure grit to make what neither of us had ever had… work. And it has. I knew within five minutes of seeing her again in person that I would marry her on the spot. She took a few days more. And we were married in aforementioned castle, exactly one month later.

We have published bestsellers together since then. We have built a small but reputable publishing company together. The same one that is publishing the book you, dear reader, now hold. And we have been through ups and downs, family attitudes and infighting, and just about everything else this world has thrown at us individually the last several years. But we have handled it together with the same faith, fortitude, and again, aforementioned grit, to overcome it all successfully.

So, to my wife and the woman I searched for all of my life, thank you from the bottom of my heart for it ALL. The logistical, and the emotional. The physical, and the poetic. The intense, and the comfortable. Thank you, Heather Daughrity, for lifting the other side of the couch so easily. I love you in ways my paltry words will never be able to describe; like a poet's words always miss the mark on describing a sunrise, I could never do justice to describing the love I feel for you. I can only show it to you…every day.

>*Mo Chuisle…tá tú mo gach rud…*
>And now for the rest of the story…

To my readers, fans, supporters, beta team, friends, and family, I thank you from the bottom of my heart. You have embraced me, and my books, in ways I never imagined, nor dreamed of. Here's to you, a loud cheer, and with raised glass, salute to you all.

To my children and all those who will come after me, please take everything you have seen in me and my life, and all that I have accomplished, and take notes. God takes us through the very heart of the fire, not to burn us up and destroy us, but to strengthen, harden, and purify us in the very things that we believe will destroy us completely.

And also to my children, all of them, biological and adopted into the Daughrity family through marriage, I love you all and miss you all. We are so very proud of you all, and hope that when the day comes that we are all under the same roof, and can rejoice and celebrate our whole and complete family, I hope and pray that you see that things had to go the way that they did, and because they went the way that they did, it made us stronger, more able, and capable.

Thank you to my core team of Beta readers, and now, new readers. Thank you to friends, old and new. If you've read, commented upon, listened to, and reviewed one or more of my books, thank you from the bottom of my heart for the support. I haven't had means to promote and market these books very much, but word of mouth from those who have read and fallen in love with these books, have taken them to places I never dreamed possible.

Other Beta Team readers included Michelle Cronin, Sarah Zhang, Tracy Ennis (and Abigail Ennis, thank you for buying my books early on and sharing them with your amazing family! I can't wait to see how our families join together!), Dianna Malone, Sherry Neil (Mrs. Neil, even when I was a child you were the best example of a surrogate mother to so many Boy's Ranchers!), Ruby Godfrey (also an amazing surrogate mother to the Ranchers), Michelle Richards (love you cousin), Shane and Angel Storrs (see you guys soon! Love you so much! And tell Cayden he only has one job!), Sandra D'Ambroise (love you my cousin and spiritual guru), Brandi (Brassy) Fox-Young, Brian Clince, and his wife, Rachel, (thank you Moose, for allowing me to use you, your family, and your amazing town in two of my books now), Katie Bitz, Krystall Williams, Katy Orawsky, Marina Aris (an amazing publisher, writer, and all around wonderful human being and mother in her own right), Michelle Templin, and many others who came and went like the tides.

There are also thousands of people on multiple platforms and social media sites that have given some small encouragement when it was needed most, and who are on the same kind of road that I have been on for so long. I do all of this for you as well. I hope that when it gets really tough, when the night is darkest, and the cold wind is shaking your bones, you can see that we can accomplish anything together. We are a global family, and what happens to one affects all others in some small way. That's always been the truth of this life. So, thank you all, my fellow Warriors, for helping me get to this place.

And finally, as I have told everyone who has come in contact with me during this entire journey, I wouldn't be here if it wasn't for God's constant hand on my life, directing me, opening doors, and straightening my steps. Some days, when the words don't come as easy as others, it's a simple meditation and prayer, and they appear like a miracle. When resources are thin, and I was trying to figure out how to keep a roof over my head, I was always provided for. When emotions and pain threatened to overtake me, over and over again, peace flooded me like a river.

Thank you all, Happy Readers, for getting to this place with me, and thank you to all those listed here, and the many that I did not mention. I will write another one of these as we go along, and get everyone in here somewhere.

And finally to my creator. My God. My savior. I can't begin to understand the way everything has gone, and the why of it. I can't imagine getting through even this last year without my faith, and the hand of the Almighty on me, and my life.

Thank you Heavenly Father for allowing me to grow, to allow the fire and the furnace to strengthen me and make me the man that can and will hold all of this together.

Thank you for the stories in my head and the ability to write them down. Thank you for the strength, determination, and the grit in my teeth that gets me through everything thrown my way, no matter what. And like Gavin did in this book, thank you for teaching me how to fight, and how to fight correctly.

I told God that if He would get me here, I would tell everyone it was all because of Him. And it was. I give it all back now, because it was first given to me.

Thank you to everyone who has watched, cheered, silently prayed for, and lifted me and my family up in your prayers. And to those who are watching and getting inspired or motivated by the struggles you've seen overcome, thank you for making it all worth it.

As I always say……Hold onto your butts, people. There's so much more to come!

Joshua Loyd Fox is the author of several novels including the ArchAngel Mission series, and the non-fiction story of his life, *I Won't Be Shaken.*

He is also the author of the upcoming *I Don't Write Poetry: A Collection"* his first book of poems, and his short stories, *The Book of the Tower and the Traitor,* a companion series to The ArchAngel Missions, can be found on Amazon Vella. Joshua Loyd Fox is an old-fashioned boy from West Texas who now splits his time between northeastern Oklahoma, and the East Coast with his wife, author and editor H.D. Daughrity, and their children, friends, and as many pets and books as they can surround themselves with.

He is also the owner/publisher at Watertower Hill Publishing, LLC, and has started his own master class series titled "Joshua Loyd Fox's Mastering the Journey."

Joshua enjoys cooking, hiking, the venerable hobby of pewter soldier casting, and can be found with a good cigar and an even better whiskey, next to a wood fire, on most evenings. He lives for his family, and the journey God has led him to the last few years.

He has been a soldier, a Master Aircraft Mechanic, a cook, an amateur MMA fighter, and most recently, has worked as an Engineer, a Technical Writer and a SME for the US and foreign militaries on missile defense systems.

Find all of his work, as well as public appearances and his master class series at www.joshualoydfox.com